The Bridal Party

When proposal planner Riley is asked to plan a pretend engagement for an Italian billionaire, she doesn't expect to step in as his fake fiancée too! But accepting Antonio's "proposal" sets in motion events that will change not only Riley's life, but also those of her mother and her best friend...

In Susan Meier's latest trilogy, get swept away to Italy with the bride-to-be as she accidentally falls for her pretend groom. Oops! Meanwhile, the mother of the bride takes on the father of the groom and gets so much more than she bargained for. And the bridesmaid goes head-to-head (and lip to lip!) with the best man!

It's all happening in The Bridal Party!

Read the bride's story

It Started with a Proposal

The mother of the bride's story

Mother of the Bride's Second Chance

And the bridesmaid's story

One-Night Baby with the Best Man

All available now!

T0284269

Dear Reader,

The The Bridal Party miniseries has been a lot of fun to write. There were beautiful settings, celebratory balls, lots of wine and handsome Italian heroes.

But Marietta and Rico's story pairs a couple so different it was almost impossible to get them on the same continent at the same time. An unexpected pregnancy forces them to slow down and really see each other—and face their fears. Marietta had escaped an abusive marriage. Rico was an orphan, a baby abandoned at a bus station.

Neither one believes in love. And why would they when it let them down?

But babies have a way of bringing people together, even before they're born. The question is, will Rico and Marietta see that their relationship is the healing for their broken hearts and shattered dreams they need? Can they drop their defenses enough to admit they want the love they're both fighting against?

I had a blast writing this series. It truly was a labor of love easing these couples into their happily-ever-afters. I hope you enjoy reading the stories as much as I enjoyed writing them.

Happy reading...

Susan

ONE-NIGHT BABY WITH THE BEST MAN

SUSAN MEIER

Harlequin

ROMANCE

Harlequin®
ROMANCE

ISBN-13: 978-1-335-21619-9

One-Night Baby with the Best Man

Copyright © 2024 by Linda Susan Meier

For questions and comments about the quality of this book, please contact us at CustomerService@Harlequin.com.

Harlequin Enterprises ULC
22 Adelaide St. West, 41st Floor
Toronto, Ontario M5H 4E3, Canada
www.Harlequin.com

Printed in U.S.A.

A onetime legal secretary and director of a charitable foundation, **Susan Meier** found her bliss when she became a full-time novelist for Harlequin. She's visited ski lodges and candy factories for "research" and works in her pajamas. But the real joy of her job is creating stories about women for women. With over eighty published novels, she's tackled issues like infertility, losing a child and becoming widowed and worked through them with her characters.

Books by Susan Meier

Harlequin Romance

A Billion-Dollar Family

Tuscan Summer with the Billionaire
The Billionaire's Island Reunion
The Single Dad's Italian Invitation

Scandal at the Palace

His Majesty's Forbidden Fling
Off-Limits to the Rebel Prince
Claiming His Convenient Princess

The Bridal Party

It Started with a Proposal
Mother of the Bride's Second Chance

Reunited Under the Mistletoe
One-Night Baby to Christmas Proposal
Fling with the Reclusive Billionaire

Visit the Author Profile page
at Harlequin.com for more titles.

I dedicate this book to all my Facebook friends who
listen to my silly stories and put up with my offbeat
sense of humor. You make my days brighter.

Praise for
Susan Meier

"*One-Night Baby to Christmas Proposal* is another
uplifting novel with equal measures of romance and
drama from author Susan Meier. I have truly enjoyed
all of her books that I've read so far."

—*Harlequin Junkie*

CHAPTER ONE

RICO MENDOZA DROVE his Bentley along the Tuscan road leading to the expansive vineyard owned by his unofficial family, the Salvaggios. Abandoned as an infant, Rico had been raised in various foster homes and group homes. At twenty-eight, he'd met Antonio Salvaggio at a meeting where they were discussing a potential business venture. When it was over, Antonio had insisted he come to the Salvaggio villa for dinner. He'd met Carlos and GiGi, Antonio's grandparents, and Lorenzo, Antonio's dad. Ten years later, he gambled with Lorenzo in Monte Carlo, popped in to spend afternoons with GiGi every time he was in Florence and was like a brother to Antonio.

He'd flown in from London two days early for Antonio's engagement party on Saturday night because he knew there'd be wine and laughter. He hadn't even been told Antonio was dating someone, but apparently, the whole romance had happened quickly. Antonio had met the woman he now described as his one true love, romanced her a few months, got engaged and was not wasting a minute getting married.

The man was smitten.

Rico snorted when he thought of Antonio calling a woman his one true love. Rico wasn't a big believer in love. But Antonio was. Though his first marriage hadn't worked out and he'd been a happy playboy for years, there had always been something wistful about him. He hadn't been lost—Rico knew exactly what lost looked like—it was more that Antonio seemed to want something different from his future.

The vineyard lane appeared on Rico's left, and he turned the Bentley onto the long strip of pavement. He'd barely noticed the fields as he'd driven along the road, but heading toward the Salvaggios' massive vineyard, he saw row upon row of resting grapevines, the huge wine-making facility and the beautiful yellow stucco villa.

He eased his car along the curving driveway and stopped in front of the enormous garage. Though he knew there were plenty of people arriving for the engagement party weekend, there were no other cars parked in the driveway.

Not wanting to leave his Bentley in the way when other vehicles might need to drive up to the portico, he pulled out his phone and texted Lorenzo, asking where he should park his car.

A few minutes later, Antonio's dad stepped out

of the villa. Tall with dark hair and serious brown eyes, he approached the Bentley.

Rico eased out of his car into the crisp December air. Given that Lorenzo wore jeans and a cashmere sweater, Rico was appropriately dressed in a T-shirt and jeans with a black leather jacket. He caught Lorenzo in a big hug.

"Good to see you, old man," he said, slapping Lorenzo's back.

Lorenzo snorted. "I'm far from an old man."

"I know. Rumor has it you have a new lady in town."

Lorenzo gaped at him. "What?"

"I know. I know. It's a secret. The way all your relationships are."

"Not all my relationships are a secret!" He stopped his little rant, shaking his head as he grinned at Rico's teasing. "Just leave your car and one of the maintenance guys will park it inside. We can text them to get it for you when you're ready to leave."

Rico tossed his car starter in the air with a laugh, then set it on the front seat. "Don't think I didn't notice you're evading the question about your mystery woman."

They walked to the front door, which Lorenzo opened, offering Rico entry first. But Rico laughed. "Age before beauty."

"You know, you're so cocky, but you're going to get old too."

"I hope so. The alternative isn't appealing."

Lorenzo snorted and entered the foyer. Rico followed him. He paused to take in the gorgeous space with its crystal chandelier and curving staircase, then Lorenzo motioned for him to go into the sitting room to the right.

Antonio and a gorgeous brunette sat on a chair catty-corner to the sofa. As Rico and Lorenzo entered, Antonio rose and caught the hand of the brunette, saying, "Riley, that troublemaker with my father is my best man, Rico."

Riley laughed as they walked over to him. "He doesn't look like a troublemaker."

Antonio sniffed. "Give him time." Stopping in front of Rico, he added, "Rico, this is my fiancée, Riley Morgan."

Rico hugged Riley. "It's a pleasure to meet you." It really was. Rico himself might not believe in love and might not want to get married, but Antonio did. It gave him great joy to see his friend happy.

Antonio pointed to the sofa. "And of course you know GiGi."

He walked over and took her hands. She'd lost Carlos at the beginning of the year and Antonio and Riley's wedding seemed to be bringing her back to her usual, happy self.

He kissed the back of her hands. "The only sweet one in this family."

GiGi laughed. "Oh, you love my boys too. Otherwise, you wouldn't tease so much."

"Next to her," Antonio continued, "is Riley's mom, Juliette Morgan."

He faced the stunning blonde with the most expressive green eyes Rico had ever seen. "How do you do."

"It's nice to meet you," Juliette said.

"And next to her is Riley's maid of honor, Marietta Fontain."

Rico eased down another step to be in front of her and said, "It's nice to meet you."

She looked up at him. Her soft blue eyes caught his gaze and his heart jerked. Strawberry blond hair to the middle of her back framed a face with high cheekbones and a pert little nose. She looked like a sprite or a pixie. Someone from Celtic folklore.

She smiled and his heart thudded.

"It's nice to meet you."

He stared at her. Her voice had the cutest accent, a sort of twang. She was obviously from the American South. "Your voice is beautiful."

She laughed. "I grew up in Texas."

She said that as if it explained everything, but unexpected curiosity about her filled him with a million questions. The kind of questions he normally didn't ask, if only because he didn't want anyone asking him about who he was. He didn't know anything about who he was, except that his mom had left him in a train station in Spain and he had the coloring and stature of a Spaniard.

Stifling his curiosity about Marietta Fontain, he sat in the thick chair across from Antonio and Riley. Lorenzo walked behind the bar and got everyone wine.

Through drinks and dinner, Rico joined in the fun, laughing with everyone as they discussed the upcoming engagement ball. Then Antonio and Riley suggested that Marietta and Rico join them in the wine-tasting facility for dancing that night.

As they entered the building, Rico smiled. Most wine-tasting rooms weren't tricked out the way the Salvaggio Vineyards' room was. Most had tables and chairs and happy employees pouring samples. But Lorenzo had seen wine-tasting rooms in the United States that had fancy bars, with backlit rows of wine, tables for conversations and a dance floor, and had decided to copy the idea. Tourists didn't merely sample the Salvaggio wines; they enjoyed the atmosphere and the ambiance of mingling with other tourists and dancing and returned home talking about the experience. As a result, a visit to the Salvaggio Vineyards was on everyone's not-to-be-missed list.

The band began to play. Antonio smiled at Riley, took her hand and led her to the dance floor.

Anticipation filled Rico. This was his chance to get to know Marietta, away from GiGi's curiosity and Lorenzo's teasing. He turned to face her, and she smiled at him.

His chest tightened. He didn't know what it was about her that made his heart stutter and his brain turn to mush. But he was not letting this opportunity get away. "Would you like to dance?"

She laughed. "Yes and no. Yes, because I love music. But honestly, I'm exhausted."

The urge to talk her into a dance, just one dance, nudged at him, but the gentleman in him won. He directed her to one of the empty tables. As they walked over, he said, "That's right. You flew in from the States today."

"And took a train and drove the last few miles with Juliette in her maiden drive in Tuscany. If she offers you a ride anywhere, politely decline. At least until she knows her way around better."

He laughed. Not only was it pure joy to hear her Southern drawl, but she seemed to be a good sport about things. "After she held her own with Lorenzo at dinner tonight, I'm not sure Riley's mom takes no for an answer."

Marietta snorted. "She doesn't. She and Riley shared office space and me. I was the receptionist and office manager for both. When she sets her mind to something, she doesn't back off."

Even in the dim light of the room, her skin glowed. But it was her eyes that seemed to charm him the most. Pale blue, like the sky on a perfect day.

His lips lifted into a smile. But as he walked to the bar to get glasses of wine for himself and Marietta, he wondered if he was beginning to feel a little bit of what Antonio seemed to feel for Riley.

Smitten.

Good Lord. He could not be smitten. Smitten was for guys like Antonio who wanted to be devoted, to have children, to be selfless and self-indulgent with the same person. Not for people like Rico who liked nightlife, who lived and breathed freedom. What he felt for Marietta was simple attraction. Nothing more.

Still, there was nothing wrong with that. Especially if she was feeling the same thing. If the attraction was mutual, they had a whole weekend to explore it.

The song ended. Antonio and Riley walked over to their table holding hands. Riley looked from Marietta to Rico. "What are you guys talking about?"

Marietta chuckled. "Your mother."

"Oh! How she and my dad have a thing?" Antonio asked.

Rico set down his wineglass. "*Juliette* is the woman your dad has in town?"

Riley batted her hands, indicating he should keep his voice down. "We're not sure yet. We've been trying to trap them into admitting it. But my mom is like a vault when she wants to be…"

"And my dad is the king of never giving a straight answer."

Rico laughed and took a sip of his wine. "That could make this weekend a lot of fun."

Antonio gasped. "Don't say anything, Rico. Riley and I have been treading lightly in the way we're edging them into admitting the truth. We don't want to do anything that might cause a problem at the engagement party."

Marietta hid a snicker by taking a drink of her wine. It would be a cold, frosty day in hell before Juliette broke down when challenged. Looking around the room dripping with finery, she took in the tall walnut tables that matched the shiny bar in front of the backlit rows of fancy bottles of Salvaggio wines. They'd made the room bigger than other wine-tasting rooms she'd seen in Texas, but she'd been to plenty of vineyards that had music and dancing to attract customers.

The Salvaggios certainly took the wine-tasting room to the next level, though. Which was probably why their vineyard was a standout in their industry. Of course, Salvaggio Wines was only one of many businesses they owned. The Salvaggios were billionaires. Juliette owned a home nursing agency. Even Riley owned a company.

Of course, she didn't know Rico's status—

Except that he was gorgeous. And yummy. Thick, curly dark hair was complemented by a sexy black leather jacket that he wore like a man so accustomed to luxury he could dress casually and still reek elegance. He was probably wealthy too.

No matter how tempting she found him though, she knew she should keep her distance. Stay in her own lane. She was a Texas girl, making a life in Manhattan, who'd barely dated since her divorce. Rico Mendoza was way out of her league.

Even if he did make all her nerve endings shimmy and her chest tighten with longing.

The band began to play again. This time a slow song. Antonio immediately led Riley back onto the dance floor.

Marietta pretended great interest in her wineglass. She'd already told him she was too tired to dance.

"Do you want to get out of here?"

Marietta's gaze leaped to his. "Out of here?"

"Antonio mentioned that we're staying in the same hotel. You're tired. I have a car. We'll wait for Antonio and Riley to get back from this dance, then say we're going to our hotel because I understand tomorrow's a big day."

She could have gazed into his beautiful dark eyes forever. "A big day for what?"

"I don't know. Whatever it is people do to get ready for an engagement party."

"We're choosing my maid of honor dress tomorrow. Maybe something along the lines of choosing a wedding tux for you?"

"I own a tux."

Of course he did. No matter how appealing, he was way beyond her. Not somebody she should even consider flirting with.

She changed the subject. "If it was summer, I'd be hoping we were spending tomorrow afternoon at the pool. Did you see that outdoor space? GiGi said she just redid it."

"I've seen it. You're right. It's perfect."

"But not in the winter."

"No. Not in the winter."

Silence fell over their small table. She worked to think of something to say. Her instinct was to flirt. But she'd already discounted that. They weren't merely from two different worlds. They were from two different continents. Best to simply try to make friends and keep it that way.

Except she was really attracted to him. Tall, dark and handsome...and just *yum* with that mop of curly hair.

But she wasn't in the market for a guy.

She'd had a bad marriage and didn't want another—

Maybe that was the answer? She really didn't want to marry again. But that didn't mean she couldn't flirt...or have some fun.

Did it?

Antonio and Riley returned to the tall table,

cuddling and happy. Marietta smiled at them, as Rico shoved away from the table. "Marietta is tired from traveling and I need to get back to the hotel to make some calls to the States."

Riley said, "Oh."

Antonio said, "Okay. We'll see you tomorrow."

"Any special time you need for us to be at the vineyard?"

"No," Riley said. She squeezed Marietta's hand. "Sleep in. Have a leisurely breakfast."

She slid into her jacket. "That sounds like heaven."

"Especially since you have your own room."

They headed for the door and walked out into the starry night, taking the cobblestone path that led to the pool area that GiGi had just redone. Instead of turning left toward the pool, Rico went right, through a garden that had a few shrubs but no flowers, given that it was December. Then suddenly they were at the far side of the house.

"I'll text Lorenzo and see how I get my car out of the garage."

She stood in the cold night, fighting a shiver.

A garage door suddenly rose.

Rico laughed. "That Lorenzo. Everything's connected to his phone."

They walked inside. He eased over to a Bentley and opened the door for her. She slid inside. While he rounded the hood, she glanced around.

Holy cats.

The villa had clued her in that the Salvaggios had more money than everybody she knew put together. But suddenly the sheer volume of wealth around her overwhelmed her. New York City, Manhattan in particular, was filled with beautiful things.

But this was *luxury*.

She didn't belong here. And she most certainly did not belong with Rico. Not even to flirt a bit.

Ridiculous disappointment filled her. She knew all about life not turning out the way she thought it should. Not getting what she wanted. She'd learned to temper her wishes and goals into something that fit her life.

But telling herself no tonight felt wrong.

CHAPTER TWO

RICO STARTED THE car and drove them to the country road that would take them to Florence. He hadn't missed the way Riley had said that Marietta should sleep in because she had her own room. Meaning, she usually slept with someone and was probably married! If that was true, it would put an end to all his unusual longings around her—and his plan to turn this into a fun, romantic weekend with the maid of honor.

Not being able to come right out and ask, he hedged a bit. "So...you get a room to yourself?"

She laughed. "Riley always teases me about the fact that I have three roommates in a two-bedroom apartment. There are two of us in each bedroom."

He glanced over at her. "You aren't married? You have roommates?"

"It's not unheard of in New York. Rent is through the roof. And I wanted to be there, in the thick of things to find myself, to make my mark." She shrugged. "I wasn't afraid to sacrifice."

He knew all about sacrifices too. Or maybe more like life necessities. "My first apartment was two rooms above a garage. Cold in the winter. And smelled like mold."

She burst out laughing.

He peered over at her. She didn't feel sorry for him? She didn't dismiss his past as something that was over so he should forget it? She saw the humor?

"The stairway to the entry was outside. Cats would congregate by my door every morning. I think the tenant before me probably fed them and they expected me to keep up the tradition."

She laughed again. "And did you?"

He took a breath. "I'm a sucker for anybody or anything who needs a little help."

"It's connection. I had a crappy end to my marriage, and two of my three roommates are women who also left bad relationships." She shrugged. "I knew exactly what they were going through. I happily accepted them when they applied. What's your connection to the cats?"

The question should have gotten his shackles up. But she wasn't asking out of curiosity. They were simply talking honestly. And it wasn't like he hid his past. In this day of technology, no one could hide their past. All she had to do was research him. Everything was there.

"I was an orphan." Which was a cleaner way of explaining his life than admitting someone had left him in a train station. Everyone assumed it was his mom since there had been a lipstick print on his cheek from where she'd kissed him good-bye. "Raised in foster homes until I eventually ran away to be on my own."

She glanced around the Bentley. "Looks like you did okay."

"I did. I jumped around, worked mostly as a waiter until I was twenty-one. I couldn't seem to get anything together in Spain, so I went to London. When I got there, I found a job as a limo driver because those guys get really great tips. A couple weeks in, I picked up this man at the airport and rather than sit in the back he sat in front with me."

"That's odd."

"He told me his daughter was considering starting a rideshare company. He wanted to talk her into getting limos instead of using the cars of people who worked for her. He asked a million questions and when he found out how much money I made, he looked at the worn jeans beneath the company jacket and asked me what I was doing with all those good tips." He smiled at the memory. "I said paying rent and he rolled into this long speech about how lucky I was to be young and if I would start saving and investing now, I could be a billionaire someday." He chuckled. "He was right."

She frowned. "Maybe I should run into him."

"I could arrange it. Not only does he live in Manhattan, but we're still friends because every time he came to London, he requested me as his driver. We'd have these great talks. He told me things I had no clue about. Like living off my hourly wage and saving every cent of my tips so I'd have money to invest. Four years later, I'd scraped together enough to start a limo company that competed with the one I had worked for. Two years after that, I was going to his business meetings with him. That's how I met Antonio. We bought a company together and became friends. Ten years and a few really good opportunities later, I'm the billionaire Ethan O'Banyon had said I would be."

"That's amazing."

He released a breath, suddenly so comfortable with her that his over-the-top attraction to her made sense. They both knew life wasn't easy. "It's really a matter of two things. Living below your means and getting lucky with investments."

"Sounds like it didn't hurt that you found a mentor."

He laughed. "No. It did not. I always considered my meeting Ethan to be life's way of making it up to me that I was abandoned."

"That's a healthy way of looking at it."

"It is. There is absolutely no point in dwelling

on the past. Making a future is a much better use of your brain."

"That was how I looked at it when my husband dumped me."

He winced. "Ugh. Sorry."

"Don't be sorry. Our marriage had been deteriorating. I just never got the gumption to leave myself." Even discussing something unhappy, her pretty accent gave him goose bumps. "Wish I had. But I didn't dwell on that. I asked myself what I wanted, and I decided what I really, really wanted was my freedom."

"Your husband must have been extremely difficult to live with if your big goal was freedom."

She took a breath. "He was. We didn't start out that way. We dated all four years at university." She laughed. "Even had the same business management classes. We were like two peas in a pod. But after being perfect together for so long, about a year or so into our marriage, his temper began to make ugly appearances when we'd argue. He blamed things on me. Yelled a lot. Then I realized he used his temper to make everything look like my fault." She paused, then shrugged. "Anyway, I was relieved when he told me he wanted to end our marriage."

Just from the little she'd said, he knew there was more to her bad marriage than she was letting on, but nobody told the entire story of their life in the first private conversation they had with someone. From the way she fiddled with her jacket and purse, he knew she was embarrassed to have even said what she had.

But she shouldn't be. He didn't condemn her for a bad marriage or even for letting details slide into a getting-to-know-you conversation. He understood having a difficult past.

To ease her discomfort, he said, "I felt the same way when I'd be moved away from foster parents who were abusive."

She winced. "Your foster parents were abusive?"

"Not all of them. But there were many who believed in using a belt or the back of their hand to get a confused kid to fall in line."

"That's awful."

"It's also the past. I guess what I'm trying to say is that it sounds like we're both survivors."

She smiled. "It does."

This time her smile didn't throw him for a loop. This time, he actually felt the softness of it. Along with a click of connection. And why not? They *were* both survivors. And not survivors who wore their hearts on their sleeves. Survivors who knew life was sometimes about moving on.

"Tell me more about your life now."

"I'm having a blast being myself."

He laughed. "Really?"

"In Texas, towns are small and everybody knows everybody. In Manhattan, I can do what I want without worrying what anybody else thinks because most people aren't paying attention."

He chuckled. "That is true. I never thought of it that way."

It was another area in which they were similar. He liked being able to do what he wanted too. Though for a different reason. She liked the freedom of choices, but he liked that he answered to no one.

It was no wonder they had a click of connection. They might come at things from different angles or with different motivations, but their bottom lines were the same.

They arrived at their hotel. Both had already checked in, so they simply walked by the noisy glass-walled bar to the elevator. She reached to hit the button for her floor. He reached to hit the button for his. They hit the button for three simultaneously, their hands bumping against each other.

At the feeling of her soft skin beneath his fingertips, he froze, then swallowed hard. Touching her—even so innocently—was wonderful. And here they were, both in the same hotel—not staying at the villa—giving them privacy and opportunity to do whatever they wanted.

She laughed nervously. Their accidental brush seemed to have had the same effect on her as it had had on him. The stars seemed to be aligning for them.

"I see we're both on three."

She said, "That's convenient," then her very pale skin turned pink.

She'd blushed?

Because she'd said that's convenient?

Oh, yeah. He understood. If they were sleeping together, it would be very convenient to be on the same floor. She might not have intended her comment that way. But once the words had slipped out of her mouth, she'd realized they could have that meaning.

The doors swished closed.

He smiled at her. She smiled at him. Attraction washed through him again. Not the simple urge when a person meets someone physically attractive. But a strong intuition that they could have something wonderful this weekend—and the week before the wedding when everyone was supposed to gather to prepare for the big day.

Living on different continents, they'd never have a relationship. But this was exactly the kind of situation that one-night stands were made for. An incredible attraction. No chance of anything permanent. Just a moment stolen out of time.

Still—

They were in the same wedding and neither one of them wanted to do anything that might somehow affect Antonio and Riley's big day. He'd have to think all this through before he acted on what appeared to be a very happy impulse.

The elevator bell rang. The doors slid open. He motioned for her to exit before him. They both turned right.

She dug out her key as they walked down the hall. He ambled past his room, continuing on with her. The hall was empty, but a person never knew if there was someone around a corner, waiting for an unsuspecting tourist. A gentleman, he decided to walk her to her door.

They reached her room and Marietta's breath shimmied. All her confusing thoughts about Rico had been banished. He might be extremely wealthy now, but he knew what it was to struggle. They were more alike than she ever would have guessed, and it was going to be a lot of fun to hang out together at the engagement ball and during the week before the wedding.

If they started something romantic, that might actually make the engagement party and wedding week even more fun.

She stopped at her door and displayed her key-card. "This is me."

"Then I'll say good-night."

"Good night."

He didn't move.

She stood in front of her door awkwardly waiting for him to leave, then realized he might be considering kissing her good-night.

And would that be so bad?

No. It would actually be perfect. She was blissfully attracted to him. That didn't happen to her every day. Heck, it had never happened. Plus, he wasn't merely good-looking. He was a nice guy. They had enough in common to be great partners for the wedding. But she was also attracted enough to him that she'd consider a fling—

But it was up to him.

Kiss her?

Not kiss her?

All up to him.

"It's customary that you open the door so I can make sure you get inside safely."

"Oh!" Her chest swelled with the foolishness of her thought process. Dear God. It probably hadn't even crossed his mind to kiss her. It had simply been so long since she'd even thought about kissing someone—and even having a fling—that she'd gotten all the signals wrong. Or gotten so wrapped up in her own hopes that she'd—

Well, she might have made a fool of herself.

She slid the card across the doorknob. The lock clicked. She opened the door and stepped inside. Before she closed it, she said, "Good night."

He paused. She refused to think that he might be reconsidering kissing her. Good grief. They'd just met. And she'd already made herself look foolish once. That was enough.

He said, "Good night."

She closed the door and leaned against it. The problem was, the man was simply too yummy.

And she hadn't even flirted with anyone in years. Worse, she was looking at this weekend and the week before the wedding as a vacation of a sort. He would be the perfect candidate for a vacation fling. But not if he didn't think of her the same way she thought of him. They might have enough in common to be friends, but that was it.

Still, they had enough in common that she could see them having a great time at the engagement party and wedding.

From here on out, she'd behave, treat him like a friend, stop all the wonderful tingles of attraction she felt around him and enjoy herself.

For Pete's sake! She was in Italy, with her best friend, celebrating a wedding. She didn't need any more fun than that.

The next morning, Rico woke and ran his hands down his face. He'd thought the whole thing through when he returned to his hotel room that night and decided it was a lucky break for him and Marietta to have found each other and they should take full advantage. He wanted nothing more than an entire day to woo her, but he was best man in Antonio's wedding and like it or not, that was where his priorities lay. He had no idea what Antonio had planned for them that day, but he was ready to be a dutiful best man.

Unfortunately, Antonio didn't seem to have anything that needed to be handled. After breakfast, Rico, Antonio and Lorenzo spent most of the day hiding in Antonio's quarters at the villa, staying out of the way of the bride, her mom, her maid of honor and Antonio's grandmother while they plowed through their planning and organizing duties.

But he wasn't concerned. He had a car and he and Marietta were staying at the same hotel. When they left the villa that night, they could get a nightcap at the bar and things could progress from there.

Immediately after dinner, that plan went to hell in a handbasket when Juliette announced she was driving Marietta back to Florence because they had some business to discuss. Something about her new duties now that Riley would be living in Italy.

Disappointed, Rico watched a movie with Antonio and Riley, who made popcorn and cuddled, making him feel like a third wheel, even though they assured him he wasn't.

The next day, the entire villa buzzed with activity for the ball that night. If Marietta had been around, he hadn't seen her. When he returned to the hotel to dress for the ball, Lorenzo sent him a text saying he would be sending a limo for him around six. He wanted Rico to enjoy the party, not be worried about having to drive home.

Alone and feeling very much like the third wheel

again, he arrived for the ball. The butler, Gerard, opened the door for him.

"Good evening, sir. I've been instructed to tell you that Antonio and Riley will be down shortly, and you should go back through the hall to the anteroom for the ballroom where the wedding party will gather before being introduced."

"Thank you, Gerard."

"My pleasure, sir."

Head down, hands in his trouser pockets, he eased his way to the side entry to the ballroom.

When he looked up, he saw Marietta standing alone in the little room that was more like a corridor. A vision in a shiny emerald green gown, she smiled at him.

"Hey."

All his thoughts of boredom and being an unnecessary part of the festivities disappeared. He walked over to her. "You are ravishing."

She snickered. In her down-home way, she said, "I bought this gown for a Christmas party last year. Riley said it was perfect for her engagement ball. So here I am, wearing it again. It's not like I'm going to see anybody who went to a charity ball in Manhattan last year."

Her Southern drawl was like music to his ears. But just seeing her took his mood from pensive to unbelievably happy.

"Well, you look wonderful."

She brushed her hand along the lapel of his jacket. "You're pretty spiffy yourself."

"This old thing?" he teased, motioning to his tux.

She laughed.

"So what have you and Riley been doing for the last two days?"

She laughed. "What haven't we been doing? First, Riley had a million little things she wanted my opinion on." She rolled her eyes. "Especially the vows. Then she wanted lunch out yesterday and today. After which we shopped. The girl wants all new clothes for her honeymoon." She paused and caught his gaze. "Do you know where they're going?"

"I think it's a secret."

She huffed out a sigh. "These people and their secrets."

Lorenzo and Juliette appeared at the end of the corridor. Rico leaned into Marietta and whispered, "Speaking of secrets."

He expected her to laugh. Instead, their gazes caught and held. Attraction rippled through him. His heart chugged to a stop. She was about the most beautiful woman he had ever met. And she wasn't just pretty. She was normal around him, as if they'd been friends forever.

Something clicked in his heart. He ignored it. He wanted this night. She lived too far away for him to worry that the engaging of his heart meant they were starting something he couldn't stop.

After the wedding, they might not ever see each other again.

He simply wanted this night.

CHAPTER THREE

ANTONIO AND RILEY arrived all smiles. Though they obviously tried not to, Juliette and Lorenzo gave off romantic vibes. Marietta could barely believe she was there, in this lap of luxury, in the private hall, waiting to be introduced.

She peeked into the ballroom. Light from the chandeliers glittered off gold flatware, crystal stemware and diamond necklaces on the slim throats of wealthy matriarchs. She swore at least four of the guests were royals.

The master of ceremonies introduced her and Rico. They walked into the ballroom to applause and proceeded over to the main table. There was a short set of steps to the platform that was raised just high enough that everyone could see the bride and groom and their wedding party.

Marietta couldn't help it. She was charmed. The Salvaggios might be wealthy, but they were wonderful people. Her friend was happy. The ball itself was exquisite. Rico thought she looked ravishing. And the champagne flowed like water.

The master of ceremonies introduced everyone again for the bridal party song that started the dancing for the evening. Rico pulled her into his arms, and they glided across the floor. The touch of his hand on the bare skin of her back sent tingles through her. The way he smiled at her filled her heart with joy. If anyone had ever felt like they were in a fairy tale, it was her. Right now. In this minute.

After a second dance, Rico plucked two glasses of champagne for them off the tray of a passing waiter. They slid through the tables, easing away from the noise of the band. When they were far enough, she tugged on his jacket sleeve to stop him.

"I know you know a lot of people here, so don't feel that you have to stay with me to entertain me. Go talk to your friends."

"I am." The way he held her gaze shot electricity through her. The man could charm the angels if he wanted. "I'm just taking you with me. I'll introduce you to everyone."

Like a couple.

She did not let her brain go there. They were partners in a wedding. He knew people that she didn't. He was being polite. But she couldn't stop the acknowledgment of how attracted they were. And how that meant something. And how she was due, really due, for an inconsequential fling with a gorgeous guy. If that's what this was leading up to, she was ready.

She smiled at him. "That'd be great."

Walking through the crowd, he introduced her to two race car drivers who were friends of Antonio's.

She shook hands politely. "How do you do."

They glanced from her to Rico and back to her again. The tall blond who'd just won a major race smiled at her. "You're Riley's friend?"

"Maid of honor. Rico's the best man."

The blond guy acknowledged that with an, "Oh."

The shorter, dark-haired man set his champagne glass on a table, saying, "Would you like to dance?"

Rico slid his hand around her waist. "Next dance is mine." He led her onto the dance floor.

The proprietary gesture should have made her wince, except she'd made the mistake of making herself and Rico sound like wedding partners when they were beginning to feel like so much more. As if they were leading up to something… And she wanted it.

She wanted this night.

After the dance, Lorenzo came over. "I'm stealing Marietta for a dance."

Marietta sort of froze, but Rico politely handed her off to Lorenzo. He led her to the dance floor, where Antonio was dancing with Juliette, and she hid a smile.

But even as she and Lorenzo chitchatted through their dance, her gaze searched the crowd for Rico. Their eyes met across the crowded room, and warmth poured through her. At the end of the dance, Lorenzo walked her back to where Rico stood and, in that minute, she knew she wouldn't be dancing with anyone else that evening.

It wasn't wrong to want a romantic interlude with him, something as special as he was. And something that could last for the few weeks they would be in each other's company for the wedding. And when the wedding was over, they would be over…and that would be fine because she had a new job to get to.

It would also be wonderful.

At the end of the night, the crowd began to thin out. Riley and Antonio came over and said goodnight. More people left. In the almost empty ballroom, the few remaining conversations echoed around them.

A dutiful best man, Rico said, "Let's go find Lorenzo, see if there's anything he needs us to do."

Taking her hand, as he had been doing all evening, he led her across the dance floor, where Lorenzo stood alone by the bar.

Rico said, "Is there anything we can help you with?"

"No. Gerard and I will close the room. I'll text the driver that you're both ready to go back to the hotel."

They laughed about the party on the drive through the dark countryside. But her insides tingled with the idea that they were about to make love.

She didn't have to say it. He didn't have to ask. They'd been building to this all night.

When they reached the hotel, the driver pulled up to the portico and Rico got out. He turned to take her hand to help her out of the limo and kept it as they walked to the elevator, where he pushed the button for the third floor. He kept holding her hand as they walked down the hall to her room. When they reached the door, he didn't hesitate to pull her into his arms and kiss her good-night.

His soft lips met hers. Delicious warmth poured through her. She leaned in. He deepened the kiss, opening her mouth to let their tongues twine. Her arms tightened around his shoulders. His tightened around her waist.

Everything was perfect, but a strange fear gripped her. She didn't want to misinterpret things the way she had her wish for a good-night kiss at her door that first night.

She stopped the kiss and took a slight step back so she could look in his beautiful dark eyes.

The urgent need not to miss this chance over-whelmed her.

"Don't go." She motioned to her door. "Come inside."

He held her gaze. "Are you sure?"

She inched over to him and straightened his bow tie intimately. "Absolutely."

Not giving either one of them a chance to think, she turned and used her keycard to open her door. He followed her into her room. As the door closed, he caught her wrist and spun her to face him, kissing her deeply.

Her entire body breathed a sigh of relief. It could have been embarrassing if she'd misinter-preted that kiss. But she hadn't and he was here in her room. He was hers for the night and she wasn't wasting a minute. She broke the kiss and undid the bow tie she'd straightened only minutes before. He reached behind her for the zipper of her dress. It slithered to the floor, leaving her stand-ing before him in her pale peach bra and panties and high heels.

She began unbuttoning his shirt. He slid his hands from her shoulders to her wrists. "You have the softest skin."

"It's my mom's Irish heritage. Pretty sure that's where I get the red hair, too."

He laughed and she smiled at him. It felt so wonderful to simply be herself. To laugh with him and enjoy everything. And that might be the greatest gift of the night because this night certainly was a gift.

He lost patience with her undressing him and took off his trousers as she removed his shirt. He shrugged out of his undershirt and briefs and she reached for the clasp of her bra but he stopped her.

"Leave it." He chuckled. "And the sexy high heels."

With a quick nudge, he dropped her to the bed. She laughed, edging away from him as he climbed on the soft comforter with her. But he was quick, like a panther, and before she really knew what was happening, she was beneath him as he enjoyed the satiny fabric of her bra and panties.

Pleasure spiraled through her. She breathed in, enjoying every sensation before she began touching and tasting. She wanted to go slowly, to take in every moment of tingling delight, but their movements quickened as each became greedy. Her bra and panties disappeared as if by magic, then he kissed her like a man drowning in need and joined them.

For ten seconds it felt as if the world had stopped. She knew for sure her breathing had. She basked in the delight of being with him before they moved again. Not wanting to miss a thing, she ran her fingers through his thick, curly hair, then her hands smoothed down his back, memorizing the texture of him as their desire built to a stunning climax that stole her breath.

They lay together as each came down from the pleasure high, then he rolled to the pillow beside hers, taking her with him, snuggled against his side.

"I knew you'd be delicious."

She levered herself up on her elbow with a wince. "You might be confusing *delicious* with *desperate*."

"Desperate?"

"It's been a while."

"Really? I wouldn't have guessed."

She laughed. "I moved to New York right after my divorce, and honestly I've simply been too busy establishing myself to date."

"Well, I'm glad you're free now. From the second I saw you, I knew you were something special and I was right."

"I'd think you were a sweet talker or funnin' me, except I think you're pretty special too."

He slid his hand up to her neck and bought her to him for a kiss that heated within seconds. They made love again and fell asleep nestled together.

Rico had never been happier, never been with a woman who was simultaneously sweet and sexy— and something about her Texas accent made her voice even sexier. But by the time he woke the next morning, she had already gone. A note leaning against the lamp on the bedside table said she had an early flight.

Which was fine. Technically, they'd had a one-night stand—

With the promise of romance the entire week before the wedding.

They might not be in each other's world but GiGi had insisted the entire wedding party be in Florence the week before the wedding. So they had seven days to be together.

He wondered if they should be open about their relationship or keep it a secret. Secret relationships were such fun. But it was also great to be openly affectionate.

Didn't matter. What they had was fabulous and it came with a natural expiration date. When the wedding was over, she'd return to Manhattan for good and he'd go back to London.

It was perfect.

Arriving in Manhattan, Marietta felt a lot like Cinderella returning to her normal life after a night with a handsome prince...but that was fine. She wasn't going back to sweeping cinders. After years of working with Riley as office manager and her right-hand person planning the marriage proposals that were the bread and butter of her company, she was the new general manager of Riley's proposal business. She couldn't wait to be with Rico again at the wedding, but she reminded herself that it was good that they had a three-week span without seeing each other because for as much fun as they had together, they didn't belong together.

Number one, she was at the beginning of a new job, the start of a new life. Number two, he was a billionaire. She was a worker bee. A smart woman would accept that, enjoy what they had, and then after the wedding put her nose to the grindstone.

Besides, once-in-a-lifetime romances were supposed to end. Right now, she had wonderful engagement ball memories and strong confidence about the rest of her life.

Things had never been better.

Monday morning, she went to the office, wearing something one step above the T-shirts and jeans she'd typically worn as the office manager. Sissy, the new receptionist, told her that Juliette had already arrived. She'd gone directly to her office, closing the door, and she didn't want to be disturbed.

Respecting that, and also knowing her duties, she went back to work. There were proposals to be planned. But she couldn't stop thinking of Rico. Wondering how he would propose if he ever found a woman he'd want to marry. She tossed that thought right out of her head because she knew the woman would not be her. Not wanting to dwell on that, she threw herself into her work.

They still had the week before the wedding to enjoy each other.

Then that would be the end of them.

CHAPTER FOUR

THE NEXT WEEK passed in a blur of hosting Christmas Eve and Christmas Day marriage proposals for her clients, as she put the finishing touches on the planning of New Year's Eve and New Year's Day proposals.

Juliette spent the holiday in Italy with Riley and the Salvaggios, leaving Marietta to manage Riley's company and the office itself.

The pace of the business didn't surprise her because she'd worked for Riley for years. She'd simply gone from being the one who helped plan the proposals to the one who did all the planning... and she loved it. It seemed like every day she was going to a party.

On January 2, with the excitement of all the holiday proposals out of the way, she realized she hadn't gotten her period. Confused, she looked at her calendar. She should have gotten it the end of the week before. Another three days went by. Still nothing. Passing a drugstore on the way to her apartment, she almost stepped inside. But that was ridiculous. Foolish. She was a week late. Lots of women had odd periods.

Except, she didn't. And for the first time in a long time, she'd actually had sex—

No. There was no point worrying about this. She'd tried to get pregnant for years in her marriage. She genuinely believed she couldn't have kids—

But what if it was her husband who couldn't have kids?

Oh, Lord. Her husband had always blamed her for their lack of children. But nobody had ever had anything checked out.

What if Keith had been the problem?

She didn't pass the pharmacy on her way home that night. She ducked in and bought a pregnancy test. The next morning, it was positive.

After all these years of never conceiving? It seemed improbable. So, she bought another pregnancy test. Actually, she bought three and used one every morning until they were gone. Because the goofy things always came back positive. After four tests, she now believed them.

She was pregnant.

The week before the wedding, Rico's private plane arrived at the airport in Florence earlier than he had planned. The Salvaggios weren't expecting him this early, so he'd tried to delay himself by having lunch before he'd left London. But eating alone didn't waste much time. Plus, he'd missed Marietta so much that he'd barely been able to focus. Was it really a surprise that he arrived at the airport early?

The Bentley he kept in his private hangar awaited him, but knowing he was early, he drove to the hotel and unpacked, wasting time again, but eventually he gave up. He simply could not wait to see her.

In the villa driveway, he texted Lorenzo, who texted a garage employee who came out to get the Bentley. With his car squared away, he strode to the front door. He rang the bell before he entered so no one would be surprised when he walked into the foyer.

Gerard greeted him with a smile. "Mr. Mendoza. A pleasure to see you." He took Rico's jacket.

"It's good to see you too, Gerard." He could hear noise in the room on the left, so he pointed. "Is everyone in there?"

Gerard winced. "GiGi's holding court."

Rico laughed. "When isn't she?"

As Gerard walked away with his coat, Rico turned to enter what he called the Salvaggios' social room. His gaze made a quick swipe of the area. He instantly saw Marietta in jeans and a peach-colored sweater that accented her pretty red hair. But just as quickly, he also realized the room was filled with women only. GiGi, Juliette, Riley and Marietta.

"Looks like I'm in the wrong room."

GiGi waved him inside. "No! No! Sit! Tell us what's going on in your life."

He winced. "Don't you have things you're supposed to be doing?"

Lorenzo's mom batted her hand. "They can wait."

His gaze slowly shifted to Marietta, who unlike Riley, Juliette and GiGi, was not smiling at him. In fact, when their gazes caught, she jerked hers away.

He thought it odd, but this was clearly girls' time. Plus, she might not want anyone to know they'd slept together after the engagement ball. He could respect that.

"I'd rather go look for the guys," he said with a chuckle, making light of the whole situation.

"They're in Lorenzo's quarters," Riley said. "Undoubtedly someone on TV is kicking a ball, or hitting a ball, or tossing a ball."

GiGi laughed. *"Si."*

"And Lorenzo's quarters are…where?" He'd watched soccer matches with Antonio, but had never gone to Lorenzo's quarters.

"Third floor," Juliette said. "Last door on the right."

"Okay."

No one seemed to think it odd that Juliette knew where Lorenzo's room was, but he said nothing. Just nodded and returned to the foyer.

He took the elevator and walked down a hall that smelled of perfume. It wasn't unpleasant. Just different. The hall to Lorenzo's quarters smelled like a woman. Apparently, he and his mystery woman were still an item—

Antonio and Riley thought *Juliette* was his mystery woman. And wouldn't that explain why she had known which room was Lorenzo's?

No. He wasn't going to touch that with a ten-foot pole.

As he had done with the front door, he knocked then didn't wait to be invited in. He opened the door and strode into a foyer that took him to a huge main room with oversize leather sofas and a huge TV mounted on the wall above the fireplace.

Lorenzo saw him first. "Hey! Rico! Grab a beer and take a seat. We found a Bruce Willis movie."

"Everybody gets beaten up?"

Antonio laughed. "Yes. And the bad guys are sorry they tried anything."

A quick glance around showed Rico there was a refrigerator in the open floor plan kitchen. He walked over, grabbed a beer and plopped down on the sofa beside Antonio.

"Don't you guys have things you should be doing?"

"I have three contracts I should be reading," Antonio said with a sigh of disgust.

"No. I mean wedding things?"

"Like what?" Lorenzo asked. "If I even make a

small suggestion GiGi goes bananas. You'd swear it was her getting married."

Rico snorted and took a long drink of his beer.

"She made us both take a week off work just so she can tell us not to touch anything."

"So you're watching movies?"

"And Knicks basketball," Antonio said. "Riley's taken me to Madison Square Garden to watch them play."

"Sounds fun?" Rico said with a wince.

"It is. We'll show you later."

He glanced around. This was not at all how he pictured this week going. First, for some reason, he imagined himself and Marietta meeting in the foyer and sharing a passionate kiss. Then, he'd thought there would be tons of prep work for the bridal party. Though now that he thought about it, he wasn't sure what he'd believed they needed to do. Employees would set up the ballroom for the celebration and the vineyard where Antonio and Riley would exchange vows. And they'd probably hired a chef to prepare the food, and undoubtedly that chef came with staff.

Wine could be gotten from the vineyard supply.

Good God he was going to be bored—

Unless he and Marietta could sneak away. Now, that would be fun. Making up a reason they couldn't come to the vineyard, figuring out somewhere to go where no one would see them, or just staying in one of their hotel rooms and making their own fun.

"Rico?"

His gaze jumped to Lorenzo.

"I asked if you wanted some snacks."

The sense of severe boredom nearly overwhelmed him. But he declined with a smile and began plotting how he and Marietta could spend the next few days together.

By the time the gentlemen came downstairs after the movie, Marietta, Riley and Juliette had taken GiGi to town for a break. According to Gerard, it had been Marietta's idea.

Rico frowned. If he were a suspicious man, he might think she was avoiding him. But he wasn't suspicious, and he also knew Marietta had a good heart. The past year since Carlos's death had been hard on GiGi. Marietta was simply injecting some fun into her life.

Lorenzo suggested they go to the wine-tasting room. After getting coats, the three men walked past the new pool area to the big building that fronted the vineyards. Lorenzo got behind the bar and entertained himself and customers by pouring the samples.

Antonio began taking calls. From his replies, they were business calls.

Had there been more than a smattering of customers, Rico might have joined Lorenzo behind the bar, but there were just enough people to entertain Lorenzo.

Rico sat on one of the tall stools by the shiny walnut bar.

When the sun finally set on the boring day, he announced that he was going back to the hotel to change for dinner.

Lorenzo shook his head. "GiGi wants everything casual this week. She'll be happy you didn't change out of your jeans and sweater."

He did his best to smile. But, seriously, boredom was killing him and damn it, he wanted to see Marietta.

Finally, finally, they went to the dining room. He took his seat beside Marietta, who gave him a weak smile. Just when he would have given her a questioning look, Lorenzo walked behind Juliette's chair, leaned down and kissed her.

Rico blinked. That was the first interesting thing that had happened all day.

Antonio must have noticed his odd expression because he said, "My dad and Juliette decided to admit they were in a relationship."

"On Christmas," GiGi said. "Such a wonderful surprise."

Rico cleared his throat. "I'm glad for you," he said to Lorenzo and Juliette. "And you too, GiGi."

She laughed. "I just love love. It makes me happy when people are happy."

Rico smiled. "Yeah. It makes me happy too."

He lied because this felt like his opening. "And speaking of relationships—"

Marietta kicked him under the table.

He jerked his gaze to hers.

She pointedly said, "If you're wondering when Lorenzo's going to ask me to set up a proposal for him, don't. They're taking things slowly."

She drew out the word *slowly* so much that he knew she was sending him a message. Apparently, his second guess for why she seemed so distant was correct. Marietta didn't want to announce that they were an item.

Which was fine. He couldn't believe he'd almost let the cat out of the bag just because he'd been bored and restless all day…and hadn't seen her.

He was simply antsy. That's all. He could keep a secret with the best of them.

Dinner was served. The conversation was lively. Especially from Lorenzo, who behaved like a man who'd finally found happiness. The guardian of the family had apparently passed on his duties to Antonio, who was thrilled to be running the Salvaggio empire—which explained why he'd made business calls while his father entertained guests in the wine-tasting room.

They took dessert into the social room. After the chocolate cake was gone, Rico finally had his real opportunity. He rose from his chair. "Well, it's been a long day, so I'm going to the hotel."

SUSAN MEIER

55

He flicked his gaze to Marietta. "I'd be happy to give you a ride."

She looked at him ruefully, but eventually forced a smile and said, "Yes. That would be great."

Because it was late, Lorenzo walked out to the garage with them. He used his phone to unlock the door, waited while they entered the Bentley and waved goodbye as Rico drove out of the lane.

At the road, he turned to the right, went a half mile, pulled off to the side, shoved the car into Park, undid his seat belt and reached for Marietta. He heard the click of her seat belt unlocking.

She turned into his arms, and he pulled her to him for a desperate, happy, passionate kiss. For a second, he was tempted to pull her onto his lap, but she shifted away.

"We need to talk."

"Hey, no worries. If you don't want anyone to know we're being romantic, I can keep a secret."

She winced. "I'm afraid the secret's a little bigger than that."

He frowned, absolutely confused about what she was talking about.

She sucked in a breath. "I'm pregnant."

All the blood drained from his body. He swore it puddled at his feet, rendering him frozen and speechless. He tried to blink to bring himself back to life and even his eyelids refused to cooperate.

"Here's the deal," she said in her cute little

Texas way that reminded him of exactly how attracted he was to her—

Except she wasn't just a gorgeous woman anymore. She was pregnant.

Pregnant.

"After spending years unable to conceive in my marriage, it never occurred to me to worry about getting pregnant. Actually, I never thought I'd be a mom."

She spoke in a rush. In his befuddled state, he couldn't tell if she was trying to get all this out or genuinely excited. But it did explain a few things about her broken marriage. She'd said her husband blamed things on her. She'd said she was happy to get away.

"I have a great job. A secure job. The only thing I need is an apartment of my own and now I can afford that. With all the hubbub about the wedding, Riley and I never actually discussed how big my raise is going to be, but Juliette did say it will be substantial. So." She faced him. "Seriously, I'm thrilled."

He heard everything she said, but simply couldn't process it because the reality had finally sunk in. He was going to be a dad? Hell, he'd never *had* a dad. At least not one that he knew. He had no clue how to be a dad. He also knew how difficult life could be for a child who grew up believing he was unwanted.

He pushed all that out of his head to think about

later so he could deal with the situation at hand. "You're happy?"

"Honestly, Rico, I'm so thrilled I could dance."

"But this was why you weren't glad to see me?"

She inched a little closer. "I was glad to see you. I simply was concerned about your reaction."

"Oh, I was surprised. Still am."

She laughed. "Imagine my shock. For the past eight years I've believed I'd never be a mom. Now, here I am, pregnant." She took a happy breath. "And at such a good point. You know… I can do this by myself. Don't need anybody's money. Don't need anybody's help."

What she was saying sank in a bit more. That bad marriage she'd told him about had left her incredibly independent. Which he already knew. But did that leave room for him? What would it be like to parent with a woman who didn't need him—hell, as independent as she was, she probably wouldn't *want* him around.

"By the time the baby's born I will be settled in both the job and whatever apartment I choose."

Another man might have been okay with that. Rico had conflicting feelings. As a guy who'd spent his life free and unfettered, her words told him she wouldn't mess with his life, wouldn't change his life. As an abandoned child, the thought of ignoring his own son or daughter sent hot arrows through him. He'd lived a life of not being wanted. He would not do that to a child.

He peeked at her. Before he said anything that might sound wrong, he needed to understand her position fully and accurately. "You're saying you don't want anything from me?"

"I don't *need* anything from you."

He felt totally and completely edged out. Even as he knew how bad that would be for his child, he wasn't sure what to say. Or even if this was the right time to discuss it. There were so many things to consider before he could even decide the right thing to do.

"I see."

"Oh, no!" Her happy eyes filled with horror. "I'm not saying you don't have rights. You do! If you want them. I'm trying to assure you that I've made my choices now you can make yours."

"You mean I can decide how involved I want to be?"

"Yes!"

"And how will this work? I live in London. You live in Manhattan."

She playfully punched his arm. "You have a plane, remember? You can come visit."

"That's it?"

She studied his face for a few seconds. "You know what? I've had days to get accustomed to this. It's also something joyful for me. I've always wanted to be a mom and suddenly that dream is coming true. I've thought things through. I'm happy. I'm healthy. I'm financially stable. And I really, really want to be a mom. Now, you need to take a few days to consider what you want."

Marietta watched as Rico leaned forward, started the Bentley again, then wrapped his fingers around the steering wheel. At first, he'd clearly been shocked. Now, the expression on his face confused her. She'd run every possible reaction from him through her brain and somehow this one hadn't made the list. Oh, sure. She'd considered that he'd be shocked. But this new expression flummoxed her.

Rico seemed like a great guy, but technically, she didn't know him. She had to be very careful how she navigated the waters of his place in her life. After all, her last connection to a man had been horrible.

The drive to the hotel was silent. The walk to her hotel room was equally silent. When they reached her door, she faced him with a smile. "I guess we can talk tomorrow?"

He ran his hand along the back of his neck. "Honestly, I still haven't wrapped my head around all of it yet. There are things I have to consider that you don't."

For the first time since she'd realized she was pregnant, she remembered that he was a billionaire. She'd laid out that she was fully capable of supporting their child herself. Surely, he wasn't thinking she wanted money from him, and he needed to protect himself and his fortune—

Righteous indignation roared through her. Of all the chauvinistic—

She squelched that thought. He was allowed a knee-jerk reaction or two. He could have all the time he wanted to "think things through." She'd made her plans. She was fine. Better than fine. She was about to become a mom. Something she genuinely believed would never happen for her. She did not want his money, and she would not let him ruin her happiness.

CHAPTER FIVE

THE NEXT MORNING, Marietta woke feeling a little dizzy. She waited until her head cleared before she got out of bed. She'd read about morning sickness and if this was the worst it got, she would be lucky. She was totally prepared to not only get through the pregnancy but to enjoy it.

She slid into the shower thinking about Rico. She wasn't angry with him for needing time. She'd even stopped worrying that he seriously believed he had to protect his fortune. Those were his choices. If he wanted to be angry or bitter or suspicious, that was on him.

But she also realized that his needing time to consider all the ramifications wasn't out of line either.

She also hadn't forgotten that if she'd had a child with her ex, he would have demanded rights far beyond what she would have wanted. He probably also would have sued for custody. In a way, that was Rico's world. He had money. He had power. He was accustomed to being in control. He could sue for custody.

Her chest tightened and she stopped her thoughts. She would take this one step at a time. Which meant she wouldn't worry about things that hadn't happened. Though, she did intend to be prepared to fight if she had to.

No one would walk all over her the way her ex had.

It took an hour to dress and check her emails. When her phone hadn't pinged with a text or a call from Rico, she assumed he either wasn't awake, or was still thinking things through. She went downstairs and got breakfast at the hotel restaurant. She sat in front of the wall of glass, so he could easily see her if he came downstairs.

He didn't.

So, she called a rideshare and arrived at the villa without him. He needed space. She didn't like awkward situations. She also didn't want them to discuss things they weren't ready to talk about. His staying away from her might just be a good idea. It wasn't like they were a couple. They'd had a one-night stand and created a child. A child she wanted very much. He could have as much or as little involvement as he wanted. And if he pushed too hard or too far, she'd hire a lawyer.

When she reached the doorway of the room where everyone always gathered, Juliette and Riley sat on the sofa, drinking coffee. GiGi was giving them instructions to relay to the staff who would be setting up the area between the pool and the vineyard for the vows.

She stepped into the room just as Juliette said, "So we're doing a dry run with them?"

"*Si*. I don't want them setting up the chairs or the trellis until Saturday morning. But we'll all be busy on Saturday morning. So, if we run through everything today, they'll know what they're doing when the time comes to actually set up everything." GiGi glanced up and saw Marietta. "Good morning."

She sat beside Riley on the sofa. "Good morning, GiGi."

"Did you sleep well?"

She smiled. "Very well." Unlike Rico, she'd already adjusted to her pregnancy and she was happy—

An unexpected thought struck her. She'd never considered telling Riley and Juliette that she was pregnant. She'd instinctively known that was something for later, after the wedding, after her job was official, when she was far enough along that it would be exciting to tell them. The news wouldn't get jumbled up in Antonio and Riley's celebration or the chaos of learning a new job.

But what if Rico wanted to tell the Salvaggios? He seemed very close to them. He might want advice.

She was going to have to chat with him about that and the sooner the better.

"We're actually getting lucky with the weather, if the forecast is to be believed," Riley said. "It's supposed to be sunny with highs in the fifties."

Marietta said, "That is lucky," as the front door opened. She couldn't see who'd entered from where she sat but she did hear Gerard's muffled voice and laughter a few seconds before Rico stepped into the room.

GiGi said, "Rico! Good morning!" Then she glanced at Marietta. "I thought you two were riding together?"

"I got up early," Marietta said. But the truth was she was happy not to have another awkward car ride with him. She wanted his decisions to be his decisions and she did not want him asking her too many questions. She wanted him figuring out what he wanted on his own. So that if they did go to court, she wouldn't have said things that he could misinterpret.

Rico caught her gaze. "Could I see you in the foyer for a second?"

She held back a wince. Apparently, he did not agree that he should make his decisions on his own. "Sure."

When Juliette, Riley and GiGi gave them a confused look, Rico smiled. "We're going in together on a wedding gift."

GiGi said, "Ooh, I know what's happening here. She probably has better ideas than yours."

Rico laughed. "Exactly."

Riley rubbed her hands together in anticipation. "Wonder what it is."

Marietta chuckled, grateful he'd used discretion but also enjoying the moment and this wonderful family, as she rose from the sofa and followed him into the foyer. He caught her hand and eased them down the hall to the elevator, far enough away from the social room that they probably couldn't be heard.

She caught his gaze. "Do you really want to go in together on a gift?"

He snorted. "I already paid for a trip to Tahiti."

"I thought Antonio had a honeymoon planned."

"Tickets are open-ended. They can go on my trip whenever they want."

"Better put my name on the card or GiGi will know you lied."

He rolled his eyes. "She still has a mind like a steel trap."

She laughed. He eased her a little farther down the hall. "What was this morning about?"

"About?"

"Why'd you come here on your own… How *did* you get here?"

"Rideshare. And I didn't bother you this morning because it seemed like you wanted some time alone to think about things. Speaking of which,

I don't want to tell anyone I'm pregnant until the wedding is over. I don't want to overshadow Riley and Antonio's special day."

Not sure if he was relieved that she was safe or relieved that they were holding off on telling people, Rico drew a long, life-sustaining breath. "Okay. Good."

"I mean, I know you're friends with Antonio and Lorenzo, so I sort of feel bad asking you to keep the secret for a while—"

"It's fine." He took another breath as all kinds of odd thoughts bombarded him about her taking a rideshare. Not that he was against them, but she was in a strange country.

And pregnant with his child.

For the first time since he'd arrived, he really looked at her. Her long hair fell around her in beautiful, curly chaos. A soft white sweater and jeans outlined her sexy little body. Her beatific smile reached all his screaming nerve endings and calmed them.

He actually, physically felt himself relax. He smiled, took a breath and said, "Good morning."

She laughed. "Ah. You're finally awake."

He shook his head. "I've been awake. Just not coherent." His smile grew. "You know, I've never asked how you're feeling."

"I've had a week to adjust to this news. You heard yesterday. I think it's normal for you to be off your game. And I also think some things should be off-limits for us to discuss. Actually, we both might want to get a lawyer."

He rubbed his hand along the back of his neck. "I guess."

"And I'm feeling fine. Woke a little dizzy this morning, but if that's the worst my morning sickness gets, I'm okay with it."

He studied her. He knew nothing about babies and pregnancy. The only kids he'd been around were those with him in whatever foster care house he'd been assigned. Now that he was an adult, children simply never entered his world. He worked in boardrooms and offices. His coffee company had a corporate office and staff. But he had a CEO running it. His primary function was managing his money as an independent investor. The closest he came to a child was a picture on someone's desk.

His nerve endings popped again.

"Look, I need to get back in the sitting room, and you should probably find Antonio and Lorenzo, unless you want to hear the back-and-forth about who should sit where during the wedding reception."

That sounded like fingernails on a chalkboard.

She was right. He needed to calm down, forget about the pregnancy and do wedding things. "I'll be going, thank you."

She snickered. "That's right. Save yourself while you can."

She turned away, but the oddest sense rolled through him. As if he should hug her or kiss her the way partners kissed when they parted. Luckily, he caught himself before he could do something so—

Intimate?

Connected?

Committed?

He knew all these weird feelings were the result of the pregnancy but that was the problem. He'd never been "attached" to anyone by anything other than friendship or sex. He had absolutely no idea how to handle the waves of unfamiliar emotions bombarding him. Or even how to process them. They sat on his skin like prickly sensations.

And then there was the matter of both of them getting a lawyer. That should have been the first thing he'd thought of. So why hadn't he?

He turned and almost bumped into Gerard. "You wouldn't happen to know where Lorenzo and Antonio are?"

"Hiding."

Rico laughed. "I would like to hide with them if possible." He pointed toward the foyer stairs. "Second floor. Last door on the left, right?"

Gerard nodded.

"Thank you."

He walked away grateful that he would spend

the next couple of hours watching a movie or a sporting event—

Or sneaking out with his two best friends to do something foolish like find a shooting range—or play paintball.

If he needed to get his mind off the pregnancy until they each saw a lawyer, entertaining himself was exactly what he should do. Anyway, the wedding had happened so fast they hadn't arranged a bachelor party for Antonio. Maybe he could get a private minute to talk to Lorenzo and set up a paintball outing and lunch.

Having something to do for the wedding took his mind off everything and as they watched a movie, he was grateful. When Antonio left the room, he mentioned the paintball outing to Lorenzo and he laughed.

"That's a fabulous idea. I'll get a few names and we'll give him an outing he won't forget."

They kept silent when Antonio returned. Eventually, Lorenzo left, saying he had some work to do, and when he returned an hour later, he slipped a list of names to Rico.

The note also said his assistant had already secured a facility for Thursday morning and had contacted the people on the list.

Rico relaxed. It was good to have something wedding related to do, not just to get his mind off the pregnancy but also to put his focus on the wedding so no one got suspicious.

The three men ambled downstairs at noon for lunch.

As always, the conversation was spirited, but rather than split up into two groups when they were done eating, they all converged on the social room where Lorenzo poured wine. Twenty minutes of looking at GiGi's seating charts ensued because GiGi wanted everyone's okay on who would sit with whom.

No one but Rico seemed to notice that Marietta wasn't drinking her wine.

Holding her glass delicately, GiGi said, "That's the final chart! No more second-guessing. Saturday is going to be amazing."

"Not to mention Thursday," Rico said.

Everybody looked at him.

"We've arranged something of a bachelor party for Antonio."

GiGi said, "Ah."

Riley glanced at Lorenzo and Rico expectantly. Marietta didn't even react.

Rico's heart stuttered. She looked worn down. She'd eaten lunch but now suddenly she appeared to be exhausted, and she'd barely spoken. She could be tired. Or sick. Or worse.

"A bachelor party?" Antonio said, surprised.

"Not so much a party as an outing," Lorenzo said. "And the only thing you get to know is don't wear good clothes."

Everybody laughed.

Rico looked at Marietta. Her face had gone pale.

He rose from his seat. "You know, if there's nothing else for us to do, maybe Marietta and I should head back to the hotel."

She finally smiled. She was definitely sick. Or something. Probably tired. He would not panic.

GiGi looked from Rico to Marietta. "You're going to the hotel?"

Marietta rose. "Yes. I think jet lag is setting in. I wouldn't mind a nap."

Glancing around the room, GiGi frowned. "Why aren't you staying here?"

Rico casually said, "For the engagement party, we were in the hotel. We got rooms there again."

"I had you staying there for *your* privacy," GiGi qualified. "But this is the wedding week. We need everybody here."

"Here?" Rico said, not liking that idea at all. Driving Marietta back to the hotel or being at the hotel was their private time, when they could discuss things like their one-night stand and her pregnancy.

"*Si.* You will stay here," GiGi said with finality. "Go back to the hotel and get your things."

CHAPTER SIX

MARIETTA ALMOST SIGHED with relief. Though they'd barely talked today, she could tell Rico still hadn't adjusted to the reality of her pregnancy. She'd also noticed the way he kept looking at her through lunch and when Lorenzo handed her a glass of wine. He needed to forget about the pregnancy, and the best way to do that would be for them to spend no time together. None. Let him take Antonio to whatever bachelor party event he had planned. Let him focus on the wedding.

Both of them staying at the villa would actually accomplish that. Not to mention cut down on uncomfortable drives to and from the hotel. Now all she had to endure was one ride to the hotel and the return trip here and then she could focus on Riley. Like a good maid of honor.

Gerard brought their coats to the foyer, and they exited through the front door to find Rico's Bentley waiting for them.

He opened the door for her, and she smiled her thanks. Now that she had a plan for keeping them apart until after the wedding, she intended to lead him in the direction of forgetting about the baby until he'd had a chance to come to terms with it. On his own turf. In his own world. Where he'd get the sense of what having a child really would mean to his life.

He slid behind the wheel talking. "I know you're probably mad at me for calling attention to you…but you looked sick."

"I'm not sick."

"Tired, then?"

"A little. But pregnancy is different for everyone. So far, with the exception of wanting a nap today, I'm fine. Maybe even better than fine."

He snorted.

"I'm serious. I'm starting a new job, running Riley's company. I can't have you calling attention to every yawn. Riley is my friend, and she loves me, but I will not put her in a position of thinking I can't do the job she promoted me into."

He drew a breath, as if considering that.

"Please. Just ignore me for the next couple of days. Not only is this Riley and Antonio's wedding week, but you're getting yourself more confused trying to make decisions before you can. You need to think this through in London, in your condo, doing your normal work where you'll have a perspective of your life so you can decide how much involvement you can logically handle. And I meant what I said about talking to your lawyer.

I have no idea what he's going to say. I have no idea what *my* lawyer is going to say. But I think before we make any decisions or have any great discussions, we should both talk to lawyers."

"You're right."

"And stop watching me. I swear I'm taking good care of myself. There is no need to watch me like I'm a ticking bomb."

"I don't watch you."

"You do."

He sighed. "Okay. Maybe a little. I'm concerned."

"And I'm telling you that you don't need to be. I can take care of myself. I *will* take care of myself."

He said, "Fine."

He didn't say another word in the car and she hoped he was pondering her take on things—especially the part about the lawyer.

As they walked through the hotel lobby in the direction of the elevator, Rico said, "I'll get my things and come back for yours."

"Or I could get a bellman to help me."

He stopped but she kept going to the elevator doors. She pressed the buttons for their floors because this time he was on two and she was on three.

He entered the elevator two seconds before the door would have closed and stood stonily silent beside her until the door opened on his floor.

He hesitated, looking like a guy who was going to take charge again, when he didn't need to. She was very good at managing her own life—even when something unexpected happened. He didn't behave the way her ex-husband did, but having someone hovering over her did remind her of those days, sending a cold shiver of warning down her spine.

Still, he wasn't Keith. While she would be careful about keeping their dealings fair, she wouldn't punish Rico for things he hadn't done.

"Go. I'm not mad at you. You and I are fine. I'm also done telling you what to do. But really. Think about waiting until you're in London to try to acclimate yourself to becoming a dad. The baby won't be here for eight months. We have plenty of time."

"We do," he agreed, though he didn't seem enthused about it.

"We do!" she said, trying to help him relax in that knowledge. "And I'm fine. In fact, I want to make a few calls before I pack. So drive back to the villa yourself."

He gaped at her. "And you'll call a rideshare?"

"Or if it will make you happier, I'll call Lorenzo and ask him to send a car for me."

His mouth twisted with the effort not to smile. "Just not with Juliette driving."

She laughed. Of all the reactions she'd suspected he might have, overvigilance was the one she hadn't considered. Still, she could handle this. "God forbid."

He sniffed, then smiled, then laughed. "All right. Your points are taken."

He walked out of the elevator. When the doors closed, she blew her breath out on a sigh. Rico was a man accustomed to getting his own way and she was a woman who'd learned a hard lesson about letting anyone take over even a small part of her life.

No matter how happy they'd been at the engagement ball, they were people who barely knew each other, who were about to have a baby together. She would be more than careful. She would hang on to her life, her independence, with both hands.

Rico headed to his room to pack, knowing exactly why he was getting everything wrong. He was accustomed to taking control, but he wasn't sure how to do that in this situation. First, Marietta wanted control. Which was fine. But that left him feeling as if he was standing in the middle of an open field with no sense of where he was or why.

He hadn't had this feeling since he was a kid, being sent to another foster home, somewhere he would probably be ignored, or, worse, beaten or bullied by older kids. And there wasn't a damned thing he could do about it.

He reached his room, opened the door and

walked inside. He hated those memories of being out of control. And this situation brought them all back. He knew Marietta was right about him waiting until he got to London, in his normal surroundings, to figure out his place with his child. But that didn't feel right. It sounded right. But it didn't *feel* right.

Nothing felt right.

With a sigh, he pulled his phone from his pocket and did the other thing she suggested, the thing a person does when their whole world seemed to have been flipped upside down. He hit the speed dial number for his lawyer.

"Pete?"

"Calling my direct line, Rico? This must be serious."

"It is. One of my female friends told me she's pregnant."

Rico swore he heard the sound of his lawyer coming to attention. "She told you because the baby is yours?"

"Yes."

"So she says."

Rico frowned. "This woman has no reason to lie."

"You know her well enough to be sure of that?"

He winced as foolishness rose from his gut and engulfed him. He was a wealthy man and no matter how sweet and nice Marietta appeared, he didn't really know her. She didn't seem like the type to pull a con, but he couldn't say that for sure.

"No. I don't."

"Oh, Rico. Are you falling for the oldest trick in the book?"

"Honestly, Pete. I don't think so." He didn't believe Marietta was conning him. He also didn't believe she was lying. Actually, he got the impression she'd be perfectly fine if he said goodbye after the wedding and she never saw him again.

But the logical reaction of his legal counsel did corral some of his emotions and infuse them with common sense. "She's a friend of a friend. Someone I'd never met until last month, but for her to be as close to Antonio's fiancée as she is... Well, let's just say Riley's not the kind of person to trust someone without reason."

"Your first move is still to have a DNA test to be sure."

"When the baby's born?"

"Two months into the pregnancy it can be done."

He leaned back. "You're saying I shouldn't do anything until we can get a DNA test?"

"Yes. Don't make promises. Don't agree to anything. Do your best to stay away from her for a while." He paused. "How far along is she?"

"About a month."

He sniffed. "Okay. You have some time before we know for sure this is your child. That gives you a chance to consider everything and decide on the right outcomes for you. Best thing to do is keep your distance until you can get the test."

"Okay." After another few minutes of conversation, they disconnected the call. He felt better. It would not be difficult to keep his distance from a woman who wanted him to stay away from her.

They barely saw each other for the rest of the week. She seemed to be happily busy with the wedding, while Rico kept Antonio entertained.

Friday night's rehearsal dinner was small, intimate. Just Riley and her mom, the three Salvaggios, and Marietta and Rico in the regular dining room, along with Antonio's godfather, Marco. Antonio had told him they had decided to keep it private because there were concerns about his mother. Lorenzo and Annabelle's divorce hadn't been amicable. Which made him think of Marietta's divorce and her attitude that he could be as involved with their child as he wanted. For as much as he didn't understand family and connections, Marietta had had them, and her marriage had hurt her.

It was no wonder she didn't want anything to do with him. No wonder she wanted him to keep his distance. The last man she'd trusted had hurt her.

The wedding party said their good-nights early. Everybody wanted to be rested for the afternoon wedding. But Rico couldn't sleep. Thoughts of

Antonio's mom juxtaposed his own mom, the woman he'd never known, and somehow Marietta's pregnancy got drawn into the confusion, along with her ex-husband.

At three, he gave up trying to sleep and went to the restaurant-style kitchen to make a sandwich. He took it to the huge center island and sat on one of the stools.

He'd be the first to admit he didn't understand family. But tonight, with fears about how he would handle being a dad rolling around in his brain, he couldn't stop wondering about his mother. She'd left him in a train station. If the lipstick stain on his cheek was any indicator, she'd kissed him goodbye. She'd kissed him goodbye but walked away—leaving a baby alone in a world that could sometimes be brutal.

How could you kiss someone, a baby, and then leave them to fend for themselves?

The kitchen door opened and Marietta walked in, reaching for the switch to turn on the light. She saw him sitting beside the island in the already lit room, and her hand fell to her side.

He expected her to turn and run. Instead, she ambled to the island. "So? Sandwich?"

"I was more restless than hungry, but I'm hoping a full stomach will put me to sleep."

She bit her lower lip. "I'm glad you're here. I was having trouble sleeping too."

"If that's a hint that you want half my sandwich, I'm not sharing. But I will make you one."

She walked over to the industrial-sized refrigerator. "No. I'm fine. I can do it myself."

"I know. You've told me that more than once."

She winced. "Actually, that's why I'm glad you're here. I want to apologize for being so bossy the other day and insisting you do what I say." She brought bread and deli meat to the counter. "It's just that I worked for years to get an opportunity like the one I'm getting with Riley's company. I don't want to risk losing it."

"You think Riley would fire you for being pregnant?"

"No." She pulled in a breath. "But she'll be a newlywed, on her honeymoon, this time tomorrow. I don't want her to worry. I don't want her to rush home because she's wondering if I can handle things."

He shook his head. "Women. You worry about everything."

"Hey, Mr. Pot-Calling-the-Kettle-Black. Until our chat, you kept watching me as if you thought I'd explode."

"Not explode."

"Then what?"

"I don't know... Honestly, I've been around pregnant women, but never for long and not one in which I had a vested interest."

She chuckled. "Are you telling me you're curious?"

"Yes. And maybe a little confused. *My* mother left me in a train station."

Her hand stopped midway to the bread. "Oh. That's awful."

"I didn't even know her name." He snorted. "Hell, I don't even know my own name. Rico was embroidered on my T-shirt. So they assumed that was my first name. Turns out it could have also been the name of a company that made baby clothes at the time. So, really. I have no idea who I am."

She abandoned her sandwich making and sat on the stool beside his. "I'm so sorry."

"I think…" He paused. "No. I *know* that your being pregnant is making me remember my situation and that's part of why I'm acting so protectively. I don't want to hover over you. I don't want to interfere where you don't want me. I'm not going to ask you to marry me tomorrow because I grew up without a family. Honestly, Marietta, I don't know what I feel."

"I get that." She squeezed her eyes shut, then popped them open. "I think my past is affecting how I'm reacting too. Except maybe while you're going a little wacky, I'm being a too guarded."

"Really?"

"My husband fell for me the day we met. He doted on me while we were at university. His marriage proposal was legendary. He didn't change over the years, but he did stop being over-the-top nice. And when we couldn't get pregnant, he started yelling at me and blaming me and making me feel so worthless it was hard for me to even go out of the house. I should have seen the handwriting on the wall and left him. But it was almost as if trying to please him became so important I lost myself. I will never trust anyone the way I trusted him again."

He could only imagine her confusion, her pain. "He sounds like a real piece of work."

She nodded. "He was. But I don't want you to think I'm assuming you're like him, and as a result I'm going overboard with rules. The truth is, I learned a very hard lesson in that marriage, and had to fight to be who I am now. I won't ever put myself in that kind of position again."

"Which was why you wanted me to talk to my lawyer."

"Sometimes things are better negotiated through a third party."

"It's a basic business principle. Always have an agreement drawn up by a lawyer."

"And if both of us have a lawyer, we'll take the emotion out of our decisions and do what's best for our child."

He nodded and eased off the stool. She'd told her story coolly, analytically, helping him to understand her side of things. But her marriage had not been easy. And while her pregnancy reminded him of his unhappy beginnings, it probably reminded her of her first marriage and not being able to get pregnant. No matter how happy she was to become a mom, those memories lingered and touched a part of her that might be healed but still had a scar.

"Let me make that sandwich for you."

She shook her head. "No. I think I can sleep now."

He smiled. "Now that things are back to normal between us?"

"Oh, honey, if things were back to normal, we'd be ripping each other's clothes off."

He laughed.

She smiled. "You know I didn't plan this. I don't want your money. I do want this baby."

"I know." She hadn't merely told him, but also he believed her. Still, the very fact that she was so honest with him made him feel guilty that he hadn't admitted he'd already called his lawyer.

He sighed. "I called my attorney the other day."

"That's good. What did he say?"

"That we should get a DNA test before we agree to anything."

"I don't have a problem with that. Neither one of us expected to be creating a child that night. So we should be sure. But I'm perfectly capable of raising a child myself. I'm not going to demand anything from you. For what it's worth, if you want to be part of our baby's life, I'm happy to have you. You're smart. You're successful. You're a nice guy. I'm sure you could teach our baby a hundred things I don't even know about."

Watching her happy face as she spoke, he wondered about that. It almost seemed she didn't realize just how smart and strong she was. Plus, he might be successful, but he knew nothing about raising a child or being in a family. He was a former foster kid who would not be where he was now were it not for his mentor. If anything, he'd be smart to let her raise their child without his input. He *wanted* his child having her spunk, her drive, her happiness, her enthusiasm.

A lonely ache gnawed at the pit of his stomach. At first, he thought it was sadness about missing out on raising his child. Then he realized the lonely feeling was actually about her. He'd missed her the weeks they were apart. He missed being the object of her attention, her affection. Right now, he'd like nothing better than to sweep her off her feet, hear her laugh, have her touch him… be able to touch her.

But that was wrong. They had a child to consider. A potential lawsuit happening between them.

He cleared the crumbs from his sandwich. "As you've said before, there's plenty of time for us to think about my involvement."

After the DNA test.

Until then, his lawyer had advised that he stay away.

Disappointment swamped him.

He wasn't accustomed to being told what to do. But it was more than that. They'd created a child. It seemed wrong to always discuss it so clinically. Through lawyers. Just to be sure they got it right.

She paused at the kitchen door. "Wanna share the elevator?"

He joined her at the door. "I can walk to the second floor." He gave her a stern look. "But you take the elevator to the third."

"So bossy."

He shook his head. She loved to tease and so did he. The empty feeling he had inside was also about the way they weren't being themselves with each other.

But she gave him that beatific smile and he decided he could not have picked a better mother for his child. She was wonderful.

After the childhood he'd had, he knew a baby needed a good mother far more than a child's father needed to get his own way.

The next day the sun glowed down on Antonio and Riley's wedding. Riley was stunning in a white velvet cloak over a beaded gown, standing in front of handsome Antonio. For a second, Marietta almost cried with joy. She knew that perfect weddings didn't always mean perfect happiness, but she had a good feeling about Antonio and Riley.

They were going to make it.

They said their vows smiling at each other, while Juliette wiped tears from her eyes and held Lorenzo's hand.

A lot of good had come from that fake proposal Antonio had hired Riley to plan for him as a way to convince his grandmother to get her chemotherapy treatments because she had a lot to live for.

Filled with happiness for the entire Salvaggio family, Marietta glanced past Antonio and Riley to Rico. So handsome in his tux.

A slight breeze ruffled his black curls and he smiled at her.

She was glad they'd had their conversation the night before. She knew everything would be okay once he adjusted to becoming a dad. She also knew he would carefully consider how much involvement he would have. Though he seemed carefree, he lived his life deliberately. There would be no judgment if he decided to ride off into the sunset.

As horrible as the last few years of her marriage had been, they had made her strong. Incredibly strong. She could handle raising a child alone.

Actually, it would probably be easier to raise their child alone.

The ceremony ended. Riley and Antonio walked down the aisle between the two rows of white chairs that were filled with their family and friends.

Marietta and Rico came together from their different sides of the aisle, and she slid her hand into the crook of his elbow. He smiled down at her and her heart melted.

He was so damned handsome. And really he was a nice guy. He'd also lived a terrible childhood. It seemed wrong to be so suspicious of him.

They survived an hour of posing for pictures and arrived at the villa ballroom for the reception. Rico helped her up the three steps onto the platform for the bridal table. Dinner was filled with toasts, making it almost impossible to eat because they raised their glasses so often. The whole room swelled with love and happiness.

When Rico took her into his arms to dance the bridal party dance, a million sensations hit her. She loved the feel of him. She loved how she felt in his arms. He was so sexy, she couldn't look at him without getting a sprinkle of gooseflesh. She was pregnant with this man's child because she was attracted to him. Ridiculously. Somehow in all the hubbub over the wedding and her pregnancy she'd forgotten that.

She drew in a quick breath to steady herself. But all that did was bring the sexy scent of his aftershave to her.

"Everything okay?"

"Yes." She actually croaked.

He laughed. "Are you sure?"

Memories cascaded through her brain. How he made her laugh. How she could be herself with him. How he'd seemed to like her just as she was—

Of course, those were all easy things to do in a one-night stand. It was simple to impress someone when you knew you weren't starting a relationship, simply enjoying each other's company.

He spun her around the dance floor, making her laugh, and the wide skirt of her burgundy-colored ball gown fan out around her.

"Just giving the crowd a little thrill."

She laughed again.

Holding on to her one hand, he released her other hand and nudged her back so he could twirl her under his arm, then he pulled her close again.

Joy filled her. He was so much fun.

He frowned. "Why haven't we been dancing all week?"

"We were avoiding each other."

He pondered that. "Ah. That's right. Shame that we missed all the fun we could have had dancing in the wine-tasting room."

It was. Not just because the break would have been nice but because she'd missed him. Missed his laugh. Missed his great smile. Missed the romance of being with him.

She held back a wince. All those were dangerous thoughts. She was having a child with this man and a smart woman would keep her wits about her. There were agreements to be struck and arrangements to be made.

The music changed, slowed down and Rico pulled her so close she melted against him with a sigh.

Her head filled with questions, she glanced up and their gazes caught. His eyes filled with longing. They were staying apart because of an issue greater than their attraction. All that seemed logical and right, except they were still in a grace period of a sort. Their baby hadn't arrived yet. They had plenty of time to come up with a visitation schedule—

Plus, he was supposed to be her vacation fling. But they'd spent most of the time keeping their distance.

Being held in his arms, gazing into his dark eyes, it suddenly seemed like a night for forgetting everything and being happy.

CHAPTER SEVEN

RICO DIDN'T LET her out of his sight all night. If he wanted to be persnickety, he could pretend to himself that he was concerned about the child that grew within her, but the truth was he liked her. He enjoyed her company and loved the sound of her laughter.

Was it so wrong to want to indulge himself?

He did not think so.

He persuaded a bartender to pour club soda into a wineglass so it would look like she was drinking wine.

She glanced at the soda, peered up at him, then glanced at the soda again. "That was really sweet."

"Just trying to make a smooth transition."

She smiled. "It's still thoughtful."

"I know. That's part of my charm." He grinned sexily. "Would you like to dance?"

"Absolutely."

This time when he pulled her into his arms, he let himself enjoy her the way he had when he'd first met her. She was soft and beautiful, and her lovely lilting laugh held just a hint of her Southern accent. He knew this was a moment stolen out of time, but he was taking it.

Right before midnight, the bride and groom took the microphone from the lead singer in the band, thanking everyone for helping them celebrate their good fortune in finding each other.

"We're leaving for the airport and our honeymoon. Thank you all for celebrating with us."

Rico glanced around. Lorenzo and Juliette had everything under control. Just like at the engagement party, he knew they'd close the room with Gerard when the time came.

He caught Marietta's hand and kissed the knuckles. "Wanna go upstairs?"

Her eyebrows. "To your room?"

"Or yours."

She didn't even hesitate. She leaned and brushed a light kiss across his mouth. "I'd love to."

As Rico turned to lead her out of the ballroom, he noticed Juliette watching them.

"Don't look now, but I think Juliette saw that kiss."

She laughed. "She notices everything."

"That's kind of my point."

"In a couple of months, I'm going to have to tell her that I'm pregnant. This way she might be surprised but she won't be shocked."

If he'd been drinking something, he would have

spit it out on a big laugh. They eased out of the ballroom, along the corridors and to one of the elevators. The second the doors closed, he took her into his arms and kissed her. The spark that always ignited between them didn't waste time flickering. It burst between them fully formed.

He slid his hands from her shoulders, down her arms, enjoying the feeling of her soft skin, and she stepped closer, deepening the kiss before the elevator stopped and the doors opened. They kissed going out of the elevator and down the hall, not caring that anyone on the floor might have seen them.

But when they reached her door, he pulled back. "You're sure? I mean there's a lot of stuff—"

She opened her door, caught his hand and pulled him inside. "We're dynamite together. And let's face it. I can't get any more pregnant."

She said it with such joy that Rico shook his head and laughed. But as soon as he closed the door behind them, he reached for her, kissing her so hard and so long that he felt lost, bewitched. But when she inched back a step, he woke up and instantly reached for the zipper of her dress. As it puddled at her feet, he shrugged out of his jacket and shirt.

She crawled onto the bed and after he rid himself of his shoes and trousers, he joined her. There was something about being with her that combined passion and happiness. He'd say it was contentment but that was too dull for what he felt. It was as if she brought sunshine into the room, into their passion.

He touched and tasted every inch of her. At a certain point, she nudged his shoulder. Catching him off guard, she tumbled him to his back, and she returned the favor. Little fires lit everywhere her lips grazed. When the sizzle between them hit a fever pitch, he took her by the shoulders and rolled her to her back, joining them in the process.

The heat was luxurious, perfect.

In a moment of unexpected sentiment, he knew he'd remember that feeling for the rest of his life. Then her fingernails scraped down his back and intensity roared through him, quickening his pace, tumbling them over the edge to oblivion.

Once again, Rico awoke alone in Mariette's bedroom. Another note told him she—again—had an early flight.

He rolled out of bed and dressed in the tux he'd worn the night before. He stuffed his socks in his jacket pocket and slid his feet into his shoes, then poked his head out of her bedroom door, glad when he didn't see either Juliette or Lorenzo. Though he had no idea why they'd be in the hallway, Rico didn't have the best luck when it came to Marietta.

He wasn't sure if she was a step ahead of him or if he was somehow looking for something that wasn't there. But no one ever felt more like Cinderella than he did searching that silent hall before he sneaked out of her room and headed for his own. Except for having both shoes, he was as off-kilter as poor Cinderella had been when she had to race out of a palace with the clock striking midnight.

For once, he'd like to know what it would feel like waking up next to her—

But that was a fool's thought. Once their baby was born, there would be nothing between them but the memories of how good they were together. In the same way that he'd never let himself imagine what it might be like to have a family, he wouldn't let himself, let his feelings for any woman, go too far. People who did that only invited loneliness into their life when the relationship died. He'd had his fair share of being alone as a child. He'd never invite it in again.

He made his way to his room, showered and dressed for breakfast. Only GiGi sat at the big table.

"Good morning, Rico."

He reached the table, bent down and kissed her cheek. "Good morning. How did you sleep?"

"Like a log." She sucked in a satisfied breath. "Riley and Antonio took the jet to Paris last night. Juliette and Lorenzo are sleeping in. It's just you and me."

Maybe it was his thoughts when he woke alone,

again, but an unexpected sensation stopped him halfway to his chair. With Antonio and Riley pairing off and now Lorenzo and Juliette, he was the extra person, again. The person who didn't fit.

He shook off the feeling and smiled at GiGi as he sat across from her. "I know. I got a note saying Marietta also had an early flight."

GiGi peered at him. "You did?"

"Probably a text is a better way to put it," he lied because GiGi was as perceptive as Juliette was eagle-eyed. "I just assumed everyone got it."

GiGi picked up her spoon and slid it into her oatmeal. "I'll have to check my phone later."

When, hopefully, he would be long gone.

He smiled. "I should probably jet back to London this morning."

"What's your rush? Maybe enjoy the day?"

"I missed a lot of things last week. I need to go home and get on my computer."

She sighed. "Everyone's always busy. Did you know Marietta will be taking over the US end of Riley's business?"

"Yes."

"She's a lovely girl."

Rico hid a smirk. GiGi was always matchmaking. "Yes. She is."

The cook came into the room and asked what he'd like for breakfast. He didn't even have to think about it. He was hungry for pancakes. Blueberry. The cook nodded and left the room.

"You two seemed to get along."

"I'm sorry...what?"

"You and Marietta. You seemed to get along."

"We did."

"There was just something about you two..."

And in another day GiGi would probably figure it out. Though she didn't know it, her intuition wasn't about matchmaking. She simply sensed something was going on between them. Everyone had seen them dancing and laughing, enjoying each other's company. So GiGi knew they weren't hiding their romance. Pretty soon she'd realize that. Once she did, she'd probably ask Juliette what was going on. Rather than guess, Juliette would approach Marietta.

GiGi was smart. Juliette had eagle eyes. He and Marietta were not going to be able to keep the pregnancy a secret for long. Rico would have to remind Marietta of how astute Juliette and GiGi were and suggest that she tell at least Juliette before it became an issue...or, worse, a guessing game among the bridal party.

Rico flew back to London knowing he would be calling Marietta. But as he stepped into his house, all thoughts of Marietta disappeared. He suddenly saw his home with a fresh perspective.

Marietta had told him at least ten times that he needed to think through his involvement with their child. Where he lived was a big part of that. He thought about his house—six bedrooms, plenty of room for a child, and close to Hyde Park. He was squarely in the middle of London's old-money sophistication, infused with new money from guys like him, who moved there to enjoy the luxury and convenience of it.

He could see a child here. *His child.*

His heart tumbled with emotion that mixed and mingled with confusion. He'd never even considered becoming a father. Somehow or other he would have to figure out what a dad did with a baby, a toddler, a child—a *teenager.*

This time his confusion was overshadowed by a sense of incompetence. He knew nothing about having a family or caring for a child. Of course, he could get a nanny. Actually, he'd *have to* get a nanny, even for short visits, because entertainment aside, he had no idea about feeding times, bedtimes, playtime.

He wondered how Marietta would feel about her son or daughter having a nanny, in a swanky house in a luxurious part of London, then realized he didn't know her well enough to answer that.

They hadn't spent a lot of time together before the wedding. And even when they were together, they might have talked a bit about their pasts but in some ways that left him with more questions than answers.

In the warm sunlight of his beautiful home, it became very clear to Rico that he didn't need to examine his living arrangements to see if a child fit his life and lifestyle. He needed to get to know the mother of his child.

That realization hit him so hard and so fast that he had to sit. But as he sat, he pulled his phone out of his pocket and called his pilot.

"I want to go to Manhattan."

"Now?"

Rico winced. Technically, he'd just gotten off his plane. Still, he said, "As soon as we can."

"Oh." There was a pause. "I'll get things rolling."

"If we have to hire another team to fly me there, that's fine."

"Okay."

He thanked his pilot, then walked into the foyer where he'd left his luggage. He was so confused about this whole baby deal that he'd raced to check out his home before he even took his baggage upstairs. But now he knew what to do. He didn't need to call Marietta to warn her about GiGi. He needed to talk to her. Face-to-face. Because he needed to get to know her. The woman who would be raising his son or daughter. He couldn't negotiate visitation or child support or anything with someone he didn't know.

Why had it taken him so long to recognize that? That was Negotiating 101. Know your opponent...or partner. In this case, they'd be parenting partners.

He carried his luggage upstairs, dumped out

the clothes from the week before and repacked.
This time jeans. T-shirts. Sweaters. Then he
pulled his Lamborghini sports car out of his garage and onto the street.

With his confusion gone, worry about GiGi
thinking things through fell into place. He had
taken the wheel of his life, so to speak. True, he
would have to be careful of Marietta's feelings,
but he finally felt like himself again.

Despite the fact that she'd arrived in Manhattan
on Sunday morning—the time difference worked
in her favor returning to the States—Marietta
went right to bed and only got out for water or
food.

Monday morning, she woke feeling refreshed.
She wasn't sick. The pregnancy wasn't exhaust-
ing her. She'd had a long week and a time difference dragging her down, but after some sleep,
she felt great again.

She dressed for work and was at her desk before anyone else arrived. She'd started her job
as the general manager of the US arm of Riley's
proposal planning company the week after Riley's engagement party. But for some reason or
another, with Riley now married and a resident
of Florence, everything felt official.

She held a Monday morning staff meeting,
sealing the deal that she was now in charge, and
returned to her office strong and in control. With

the stress of the wedding and telling Rico about the baby gone, energy and confidence infused her.

Her phone buzzed. She hit the button to activate the intercom. "Yes?"

"There's a gentleman here to see you. Rico Mendoza?"

Her heart stopped, then jumped to double time. She didn't even let herself wonder why he might be there or what the heck he wanted. Damage control became the priority.

"I'll be right there."

She bounded out of her chair and up the hall to Sissy's desk. When she saw him, her breathing stuttered and happiness tingled through her. She couldn't believe it had only been a day or two since she'd seen him. If she closed her eyes, she could remember the pure joy of lying in his arms.

Reminding herself of damage control, she stopped those thoughts.

"Rico!" With a smile, she faced Sissy. "Rico was the best man in Riley's wedding."

Sissy smiled, her gaze shifting from Rico to Marietta and back again.

Trying to make it appear they had business to discuss, she held out her hand for Rico to shake. One of his eyebrows rose, questioning her without saying a word, but he shook her hand.

"It's nice to see you again, Marietta." He nudged his head toward the hall. "Can we have a minute alone?"

Still working to throw Sissy off track, she said, "Oh, do you want us to plan a marriage proposal for you!"

His already confused face shifted again. "No. But there is business we need to discuss."

She motioned for him to follow her down the hall. "I'm guessing that means you have vendor names for me?" she all but shouted, hoping to give credence for why he was at their office.

They walked inside the nice-sized room with the white blinds and bleached wood desk, and she closed the door.

He didn't waste a second. "GiGi is going to figure this out."

She eased over to her desk. "Figure what out?"

"That we're pregnant."

She fell to her chair. "I don't see how."

"You know how Juliette's got the eagle eye?"

"Yes."

"Well, GiGi has instincts, intuition. At first, I thought she was trying to matchmake us at breakfast on Sunday morning. Then I realized it was more. I could all but see the wheels spinning in her brain."

"But we did nothing for GiGi to suspect we're sleeping together!"

"This isn't about sleeping together… It's about her sensing something unusual going on between us. Once GiGi starts pondering, her brain will veer off in the direction of wondering why you were tired the day she insisted we all stay at the villa. After jet lag, pregnancy is bound to be one of her options."

Marietta sat back in her big chair.

"If we force her and Juliette to guess, we become gossip. If we tell them, we control the narrative."

"Spoken like a true businessman."

"Sometimes it's good to handle things like a businessperson rather than two people who really like sleeping together. Telling them ourselves, we can take out the emotion of our situation and deal with facts."

She thought about that. "I like that."

"I do too. I'm not good with secrets."

"You can't keep a secret?"

"I don't like secrets. It's one thing to hold back information on a new product until you beat your competitor to the market. It's another to not talk about a child."

Her breath froze in her lungs. Of course he felt that way. His whole life was a mystery. A secret. Something he didn't know and might never know.

She swallowed. "Okay. I'll make an announcement."

He glanced around. "Here?"

"Juliette and Lorenzo are coming back to Manhattan tomorrow. If I know Juliette, she won't even take a nap to adjust to the time difference. She'll take a car from the airport to the office."

"We can tell her then."

She frowned. "I hadn't pictured you being in on the announcement."

"Why not?"

"Why?" She rose from her seat, walking around the desk and leaning her butt against it to speak frankly with him. "Rico, I'm running Riley's company, but I still do some managerial things for Juliette. I need the conversation to be professional. I don't want us to look like two kids telling their parents they gave in to their urges and made a baby. For me, this child is the chance of a lifetime. If I tell Juliette myself, I can make her see that, and also call upon her own memories of having Riley...working through her pregnancy and while she had an infant at home—"

"And with a guy in the room, you can't?"

"No. I just don't want to look like two teenagers confessing to their mom."

He snorted. "You have some strange ways of looking at life."

She gaped at him. "Really?"

"You might say things through that cute little accent but that doesn't make them normal."

"You mean you can stick your boots in the oven but that don't make 'em biscuits?"

He laughed. "Sort of." He sucked in a breath. "I have a deal to propose."

"I'm listening."

"You tell Juliette. I'll tell Lorenzo."

She pondered that. "What are you going to say?"

"That we're having a child and we're thrilled, and then I'm going to suggest he and I have a shot to celebrate."

She frowned. "Are you thrilled?"

"I looked around my house when I got back to London, and I realized there was plenty of room for a child. And I had some…feelings."

"Feelings?"

"Okay, at first it was fear. I never had a dad, and my memories of my foster dads are vague, except for the bad ones. So, a little panic set in. But this is also *my* child, not just yours. And no one knows as well as I do how much a kid needs parents."

She squeezed her eyes shut. "Yeah." She popped them open, then said, "Meaning you want to be a part of our child's life."

"Maybe a big part."

She could picture him at their baby's birthday parties, baseball games and even reading to him or her, and warmth filled her. But she squelched it. All her warm, fuzzy feelings for him were supposed to stop after the wedding. This was never supposed to be a long-term relationship. She'd been married. She knew it wasn't right for her. Anything between them had to be platonic, which meant she had to set some boundaries.

She shoved herself away from the desk with

a heavy sigh. "Don't forget, you live on another continent."

"As you already pointed out, I have a plane."

"Your work is in Europe."

"My coffee company headquarters are in Europe. I hired a CEO to run it. I'm primarily an investor. With the internet and conference calls, I can carry on business from anywhere."

Realizing she wasn't going to dissuade him, she looked at the ceiling. "We really weren't supposed to have these kinds of conversations until we talked to our lawyers."

"I don't think there's any harm in discussing the basics. It might even be good to have a few things decided before we drag the lawyers into it."

"You're missing my point. I'm not *ready* to talk about any of it."

"Yeah, well, I wasn't ready to hear you were pregnant the first day we arrived for the wedding. I was expecting five days of wine and romance. I might not have handled it well, but I handled it. Now, it's your turn to adjust."

CHAPTER EIGHT

MARIETTA STARED AT Rico and he held her gaze. He was not backing down. No matter how cute she looked in her comfy work clothes and how badly his sizzling attraction to her wanted to be given free rein. They were about to be parents. Getting to know each other was more important than attractions or legal issues.

Though right now the attraction really, really wanted to take over. He'd give half his portfolio if he could kiss her.

He sucked in a breath and put his mind on their discussion. This was the one he really needed to win. "And here's another little something for you. I think our next step is getting to know each other."

Her face fell. "I think we already know each other."

"No. I'm talking about getting to know each other as parents. No matter how this shakes out, we have to trust each other. And trust requires that we know more about each other than whether our ribs are ticklish."

She rolled her eyes.

He wasn't offended. After their kitchen chat in the middle of the night, he understood why she was so protective of her independence. But he could not raise a child with someone he didn't know.

Neither could she and eventually she'd see that.

"I'm here to spend time with you." He paused a fraction of a second. "What do you want to do tonight?"

She groaned. "Seriously?"

"Yes."

"Fine." She glanced at her calendar and frowned. "I can't do anything tonight. I have plans."

He raised his eyebrows. "Date?"

"With a real estate agent. One of the things that kept me from panicking about the baby was knowing I could now afford my own apartment."

"Okay! I'll come with you. There's no better way to get to know someone than to see how they choose a house."

She looked as if she wanted to argue but relented, crossing her arms and saying, "Fine," again.

He rose. "Text me where you want to meet and the time. I can come to your current apartment or meet you here."

She winced. "Neither. I'll text you the address

of the first condo I'm looking at. You can meet us there."

"Okay." He smiled. "See you then."

She sighed as if put upon. "See you then."

He left her office realizing that while he would have been very happy to take her to bed and let this discussion be pillow talk, she'd erected some barriers. Again, he remembered her bad marriage. She wanted a platonic relationship and he understood all her reasoning. He really didn't want anything permanent either. All the same, they did have to get to know each other—which was why he was in Manhattan. To get to know her.

Surely, they could fight off one little sexual attraction.

Stepping out into the cold morning, he realized he had most of the day to kill. This wasn't like being in Florence. She had a job to do, and it was important to her that she do it right. She couldn't play hooky with him. Their time together would be limited to evenings.

He glanced at his watch, then went back to his hotel, pulled out his laptop and began researching a potential investment.

Around four o'clock, his phone pinged with a text. He was to meet Marietta and her real estate agent at six thirty at a condo building. He answered that he would be there and immediately began researching the area in which she was considering purchasing a condo.

It wasn't bad. It certainly wasn't anything like his house in Connaught Village. But it was typical New York. An old brick building near a coffee shop, newspaper stand and tiny convenience store. He wouldn't criticize. He knew how expensive real estate could be.

He met Marietta and Artie Rosen outside the unremarkable front entry for the building. There was no elevator, only stairs to the fourth floor. But it was clean.

The agent unlocked the door. "Tenants just moved out and the owner decided to sell rather than rent it again. You're the first to see it."

He opened the door and Marietta sighed with surprise as she stepped inside. "Wow. It's bigger than I thought."

"Two bedrooms. Just what you asked for."

The kitchen, dining space and living area were all one big room. Rico walked in slowly. "Everything needs to be painted."

Artie grinned. "That's why they're selling rather than renting again. Buyer will have to paint…but isn't that what you want?" he asked dreamily. "To make it your own? To put your stamp on it."

"Will the price be lowered to accommodate that?" Rico asked, slowly examining the big room.

"Let's have a look at the two bedrooms," Artie said, craftily ignoring Rico's question. Meaning, there probably was no wiggle room on the price.

They eased over to the first door. Artie opened it on a decent-sized room. The closet was tiny.

Marietta nodded with approval. Rico said nothing.

The second bedroom was only big enough for a twin bed. That closet was smaller than tiny.

"You're going to need cabinets to compensate for the size of the closets."

Artie smiled.

Marietta frowned. "I already have one…from the apartment I'm renting now."

"Buying is so much smarter than renting," Artie said, always the salesman. "You're building equity and New York real estate prices never fall. They always rise. No matter when you buy, in ten years you can expect to make a profit when you sell."

The single bathroom was in a corner off the kitchen. It was so small only one person could fit at a time. Marietta nodded. Rico held back a grimace.

When they'd seen the entire space, Marietta sighed happily. "This is lovely." She glanced around the open floor plan approvingly. "But I'm not making any decisions until I see a few places. Let's move on to the second condo."

The second condo was smaller than the first and more expensive.

"Exactly how much money do you have to spend in this city to get a decent space?" Rico asked Artie as they clamored down the five flights of stairs leading to the entryway that Artie had the audacity to call a lobby. "Something that doesn't need to be painted and has a bathroom bigger than a steamer trunk and an actual lobby. Maybe a doorman."

"For two bedrooms in a more secure building you have to come up with at least—"

He said a number that made Marietta look sick, but she pulled herself together. Totally ignoring the idea of a more expensive condo, she said, "Let's move on to condo number three."

Number three was a slight improvement. But all three condos had very little closet space, small bathrooms and a second bedroom that was barely large enough for a twin bed.

Because it was close to nine o'clock, Artie told them he had three other places lined up for them to see the following evening.

Marietta said, "Thanks. Let me have a look at my schedule and we can arrange to meet."

Artie turned right and walked away.

Rico sighed. "We need to regroup."

"We?"

"Marietta, if you were getting a condo for yourself and you liked to paint and you could use the second bedroom as a closet, I'd be cheering you on right now. But you're going to be carrying your groceries and a baby up four flights of stairs. There are logistics to consider."

"Money is a bigger issue." She sighed. "Maybe I should rent?"

"Or maybe I could help you with the purchase price. If you let me add enough money to double your budget, I'll bet we could get you something with an elevator in a better part of town."

She gaped at him. "This is a great part of town. You're just accustomed to fancy things like the Salvaggio villa."

"Don't insinuate I'm a snob. I was perfectly content in that little hotel we stayed at in Florence."

She glanced away, then glanced back. "I knew this was going to happen."

"What?"

"You're not letting me be me. Any one of those three places would have been okay. But you have so much money that you forget that this is how the rest of us live." She huffed out a sigh. "My probably also unworthy apartment with my friends is just around the corner." She shook her head in dismay. "That's why I wanted to move into this part of town. I like it here." She turned away. "I'll see you tomorrow."

She left him standing on a street that was well lit and had enough foot traffic that he wasn't worried she'd be mugged walking around a corner. But he discreetly peered around the building to see where she went. She entered an older brick building and disappeared up a set of steps.

The condos he'd insulted were exactly like where she currently lived. No wonder she'd been so upset.

He hadn't meant to sound like a snob. He also hadn't meant to disparage the way she lived. What he needed to do was view this area in the daytime. He'd probably see that it was safe and perfectly acceptable.

He'd certainly lived in worse places. He of all people should understand.

Except this was where his child would live. And he did think it would be more convenient for a woman with a baby to have a building with an elevator. That wasn't snobbery. That was common sense.

He pulled out his phone to call a cab. He could plead ignorance of the real estate market in New York and apologize the next day. But right now, he wanted to get back to his hotel, order room service and investigate other condos being offered in the city.

The last thing he would ever do was lord his money over anyone. Yet somehow that was exactly how she'd taken it. While he absolutely wanted to help her with her house hunt—financially as well as with his negotiating expertise—he would have to be very careful how he proposed anything.

He supposed he should be happy that the first

crack in their relationship came over a piece of real estate rather than how they'd raise their baby—

Except technically this was a disagreement over how they'd raise their child. He wanted a say in where she lived.

And with her independent streak, he had a feeling that things were going to get ugly. Because he could be as stubborn as she was.

Marietta stood back the next day as Juliette returned to hugs and happiness from her staff. It wasn't that the employees of Juliette's home nursing agency and Riley's proposal planning company didn't like Marietta. It was more that everyone adored Juliette. And everybody wanted to talk about the fun and fabulous wedding they'd attended in Italy. Half of them had never expected to leave the continental United States in their lifetime. Getting to go to a villa in Florence? That had been a dream come true for most of them.

It was after five o'clock by the time Juliette worked her way to Marietta's office. She flopped into the chair in front of Marietta's desk.

"Things look like they are running smoothly."

"They are," Marietta assured her. "You have a great staff. They rarely come to me for anything. And managing Riley's proposal company is like a dream. I love the creativity of it."

Juliette sat up. "Oh, no. You said that so fast that I know there's a *but*! Marietta, if you found a better job, I swear I will pay you anything you want to stay."

Marietta laughed. "I haven't. I'm not even looking for another job. But I am looking for an apartment. A condo to buy. I set my budget and looked at some condos last night, but I think I set my price too low."

"Well," Juliette said. "We also haven't discussed your raise for taking over Riley's company and managing the office for both of us."

"This isn't a ploy for me to get more money," Marietta quickly assured her. She pulled in a breath and chose her words carefully. "I love this job. *Love it.* Juliette, I waited my whole life to find a job like this. I may never leave you and Riley."

Juliette laughed. "Thank you. But I did come to your office to discuss your new salary." She named a figure that made Marietta sit back in her chair. Not relaxing, but sort of in shock.

"That's a great number."

"Marietta, our situation works because Riley and I spent a lot of years establishing our companies. Now, both of us want to have more free time. Your knowing our businesses so well makes that possible. You've earned this raise."

Marietta swallowed hard. "Thank you. It's good to feel appreciated."

"You are appreciated, and Riley and I are very happy. This situation works."

It suddenly seemed like the best time to tell Juliette she was pregnant, even as it seemed like the worst.

Could she piggyback a complication onto a compliment—a vote of confidence? Wasn't that like taking advantage?

She sucked in a breath.

Juliette shook her head. "Okay. Before you have a heart attack, I know there's something else going on. I sensed it the week before the wedding. So just tell me."

Remembering what Rico had said about GiGi and Juliette guessing and speculating, Marietta knew what she had to do. "I'm pregnant."

Juliette's mouth fell open. "I thought you couldn't have kids?"

"Turns out I can." She laughed. "I mean, I haven't been to a doctor yet, but I took four pregnancy tests and all of them were positive."

Juliette winced. "Those tests are pretty accurate. But you know what? Maybe don't do anything drastic until you go to your doctor."

She laughed and almost said that's the same advice Rico's lawyer gave him. But she caught herself...then wondered why. Somewhere in Manhattan Rico was probably telling Lorenzo right now. That was the deal they had made.

"You're happy?"

"Juliette, it's the most amazing feeling to have

something you believed could never happen suddenly happen."

"I feel that way about Lorenzo. I honestly thought I'd never find real love. Oh, I knew I could have romance and boyfriends, but I thought love was something that I wasn't meant to have. And when Lorenzo and I clicked, it was like the world opened up for me and everything changed."

"That's exactly how I feel! So different. So happy." She paused, then grinned. "I'm going to be a mom."

Juliette laughed. "It's a lot of work being a single mom."

"I'm ready."

"I think you are."

"You trust me to run this place and be a mom?"

Juliette rose. "I *created* this place while I was raising Riley. All you have to do is run it. So yes. I trust you."

She turned to leave but Marietta stopped her. "Wait. There's one more thing."

Juliette faced her.

"Rico is the baby's father."

Juliette returned to the chair so she could sit. "Oh, my goodness."

"Yeah. He's kind of irresistible."

"I can imagine."

"And he's adjusting to the news."

"I'd hope so."

"And we're seriously trying *not* to make too

many plans or decisions until the pregnancy is further along."

"I'd say that's smart."

Marietta studied Juliette. She'd expected shock. But once that wore off, she'd thought Juliette would start rattling off advice. Since she hadn't, Marietta worried something was wrong. "Now, I know there's something *you're* not saying."

Juliette said, "Okay. You're right. I've heard stories about Rico from Lorenzo and Antonio." She sighed. "He's such a playboy."

"That's fine. I don't want to marry him. I'd also probably like it better if he'd let me raise this child alone—"

"He's not going to do that."

"He hasn't figured out yet what he's going to do."

"Trust me. Rico might be a runaround, but once this pregnancy and baby become a reality… He's going to want a part in things. Lorenzo told me he was raised in foster homes. It will be difficult for him to have a child and not be involved in his life."

Remembering his mood the night they'd talked in the kitchen—talked about his mother abandoning him—she knew that was true. Suddenly his unexpected appearance in Manhattan made sense.

"You're going to have to play this right. He works in Europe now because it's what he's accustomed to. But his 'work' is investing. He can do that from anywhere."

"You're saying I need to set boundaries?"

"No. I'm saying you need to establish a friendly, amicable relationship now, before the baby is born, so that when you start negotiating child support and visitation, you'll know each other well enough to be fair."

"He *is* here in Manhattan because he said we need to get to know each other."

"Exactly. He's finding his way. He might not know how he fits, but he knows he's going to want to be part of all of this. And if you're smart, you'll let him in. Show him he can trust you. So he doesn't have to move next door or file a lawsuit to get to see his child. Things like that will make you bitter enemies. Raising a child will go a lot easier if you're friends. He's looking for trust." Juliette rose. "Marietta, you are the most trustworthy person I know. Riley and I both adore you. You can make him trust you too."

Marietta sat up. "I can."

"Yes, you can." She headed for the door, but stopped and faced Marietta again. "And no sex. Seriously, your situation now is very delicate. Don't muddy the waters with a romance that will disrupt any good parenting things you set up."

When Marietta didn't respond, Juliette said, "You said you don't want to marry him."

"I don't want to marry anyone. Ever. Not ever again."

"Then do yourself a favor, do Rico a favor, do your baby a favor…and walk away from the romance."

CHAPTER NINE

RICO CALLED LORENZO and suggested they meet.
Now that Lorenzo lived with Juliette in Manhattan, he didn't have to fly to Italy. He could meet
him somewhere in town.

Twenty minutes later, he found the Irish pub
a few streets up from his hotel that Lorenzo had
suggested. Marietta hadn't texted with the addresses for that night's condo viewings, so he was
fairly certain he might have lost his real estate
privileges with her.

He pushed on the heavy door and walked into a
room that could have been located in Dublin. The
wood of the bar and surrounding tables was dark
and heavy. Pictures of Ireland and commemorative plaques hung on the walls. The place smelled
deliciously of beer and bread.

Lorenzo already had a table and waved him
over.

Removing his jacket, Rico sat with a sigh.

"What was so important that you had to see me?"
He didn't waste a second with platitudes or

greetings. That wasn't the kind of relationship he and Lorenzo had. He jumped right in. "Marietta's pregnant and the baby is mine. At least I think the baby is mine. She said she hadn't been with anyone in a while…so though my lawyer thinks I need to wait for DNA I'm inclined to believe her."

Lorenzo absorbed all that. "Marietta doesn't date much. At least she hasn't in the time I've been living with Juliette. But more importantly, she's a very honest, genuine person." He laughed. "And funny. Don't get me started on the accent and metaphors about putting your boots in the oven or how you can be all hat and no cattle."

Rico couldn't help it. He burst out laughing. "I've been warned about putting my boots in the oven, but I hadn't yet heard the one about the hat and the cattle."

Lorenzo shook his head. "So? You okay?"

"I'm gobsmacked. Apparently, her first marriage fell apart because she couldn't get pregnant, so she's thrilled about becoming a mom. I, on the other hand, know nothing about being a dad."

Lorenzo batted his hand. "I raised Antonio alone. I know you can handle it."

"You do?"

"Piece of cake."

Rico ran his hands down his face. "I hope you're right."

"Of course I'm right. And if you get into trouble, you can always ask me questions. Or GiGi. She's a font of advice. You'll be fine."

"Okay."

"So…shots to celebrate or maybe a little champagne?"

Before Rico could reply, his phone pinged with a text. "It's Marietta. She sent me the address of the next condo we're looking at."

"The next condo you're looking at?" Lorenzo's eyes narrowed. "You're moving in together?"

"No. She wants to leave the apartment she shares with three other people and purchase a place with a second bedroom."

"And are you buying it for her?"

"I wish. She wants something she can afford so she's looking in some rather sketchy places."

"Let me call Juliette and tell her to up Marietta's raise."

Rico rose and plucked his jacket from the back of the chair. "Do not do that. I might not know Marietta well, but I can tell you she's wildly independent."

"A bad marriage will do that to a person."

Realizing Lorenzo knew that all too well because of his own bad marriage, Rico hid a wince. "Which is exactly why I've stayed away from serious relationships."

"It's also why you should step back a bit from Marietta. If you want to be involved in your child's life, you need to prove to her right now that she can trust you. And part of that is being as neutral as possible."

"Neutral?"

"Don't be her best friend and for God's sake, end anything romantic. With only your parenting relationship between you, you can be open and honest and even debate the best things for your child. Romance just messes everything up. Stay neutral. It took a long time to get to a good place with Antonio's mom after our divorce. It wasn't until I dropped any sort of attempt to be friends with her and dealt with her only as Antonio's second parent that I could win arguments with her and do what was best for Antonio."

"Okay." Everyone knew Lorenzo's first marriage and his relationship with Antonio's mom had been difficult, so obviously his advice was solid.

Rico walked out of the pub, into the freezing cold January night, realizing that married people might be able to be romantic and raise their children because they had a commitment. Not just to each other, but to their family. But two strangers? Raising a child? Neutrality really did seem to be the best way to go.

He hailed a cab and arrived at the location of the condo Riley would be looking at. Surprised, he got out of the cab, peering around at the white brick building with a row of terraces up the center of the front wall.

Huge glass doors opened for him as he stepped up to the lobby—with a doorman who nodded as Rico walked into the open space furnished with modern decor.

Wearing a pretty white wool coat and a pink beret, Marietta met him in the center. "Well?"

"It's great!"

She laughed. "Juliette made my raise official tonight. But I also realized that you'll probably want to pay child support and the condo for our baby would be the best place to spend it. So I had Artie shift gears and look for a place more like what you suggested." She glanced around happily. "Do you like it?"

"Yes! Yes to child support and yes to this building!" Relief swamped him. "Let's go see this place." He almost put his arm around her shoulders to guide her, but remembering what Lorenzo said, he stopped that thought. He didn't let himself dwell on how cute she looked in a beret. Didn't let himself notice or react to anything about her.

No matter how difficult it was.

They met Artie on the way to the elevator—or, bank of elevators. There were actually three. Two for regular residents and one that went only to the penthouse. The little car took them smoothly to the fourth floor. They walked out into a wide, clean, carpeted corridor and passed two doors before Artie jangled some keys and granted them entry to the condo.

Marietta looked around at the open floor plan—kitchen, living room and dining area—with a sigh. Rico examined the space more carefully. The building was relatively new. Everything had recently been painted.

She turned to him with a happy smile. "There's a view!"

Artie motioned to the three-paneled glass door to the terrace. "As you can see, there will be a lot of light in the daytime."

A pale sofa and two chairs sat in front of a sage green tiled fireplace. A print area rug pulled the mishmash of colors and styles together.

Marietta turned from the living space toward the white kitchen. "This is lovely."

Rico said, "It really is."

She laughed. "Don't gloat."

"I'm not gloating but I might be giddy."

"With relief, I hope." She walked toward the kitchen. "I simply didn't have a good handle on finances last night. Today, I do."

He desperately wanted to hug her. Not just for pulling everything together in her mind and realizing her next step, but because she was cute, proud of herself and gloriously happy. That expression always made him want to kiss her.

Remembering Lorenzo's advice, he knocked that idea out of his brain and kept things neutral. "Let's get a look at the bathroom and closet space."

"There are two bathrooms," Artie happily announced. "One for guests and a private bathroom for the primary suite." He led them down the hall, showing them the guest bathroom, which had been recently updated, and then walked them to the primary suite. "The closet's not amazing, but it's big enough." He laughed. "Certainly bigger than what we saw yesterday."

Artie showed them three more places, all in the same neighborhood. The streets were well lit. The buildings had elevators and a doorman. Each had a primary suite with a private bathroom. Two had fireplaces.

Marietta could have chosen any one of them, but she didn't want to make a quick decision. She thanked Artie, told him that any of the four they'd seen that night would be perfect, but she wanted a day or two to consider all her options.

He saluted and left her and Rico standing on the street.

Watching him go, Rico said, "Did you tell him who I am?"

She shook her head. "He didn't seem concerned. He could have thought you were my boyfriend or my brother." She shrugged. "He's only interested in selling me something. Not my private life."

Remembering what Juliette had said about establishing trust, she waited a beat, then said, "What did you think?"

"Exactly what you did. That any one of the condos we saw tonight would be perfect." He smiled congenially. "You choose."

An odd suspicion tingled up her spine. She knew he was a nice guy, but he was also a bossy guy. A lot like Juliette, who didn't hesitate to give her opinion about everything. Still, Juliette was also usually right. When she said this was a time for her to let Rico know he could trust her, Marietta recognized that probably was the thing to do.

"I'm going to take a day or two to think through the advantages and disadvantages of each condo. Then I'll talk to my banker."

"I could finance it for you," Rico said, then he winced. "Sorry. I don't want to be pushy. I also know that getting a mortgage will help your overall credit score. You do what's best for you."

Her suspicion that something was up with him grew. Of course, he could have realized that he'd been out of line the night before and simply be pulling back because he'd learned his lesson.

But maybe that was part of how they were building trust? Making and fixing mistakes. Trying things. "Okay. I'll need a few days. I'll call you when I decide."

He shook his head. "This will be *your* home. You don't have to call. I trust you to make the choice that's best for you."

Aha! It *was* about trust. Once again, Juliette's

observations of the situation were right on the money.

Before she could say anything, her stomach rumbled loudly.

Rico took a step back. "You know what? You're hungry and we're done looking at condos. I'll let you go so you can get dinner."

He turned away quickly and started striding down the street. But as she blinked in surprise, he faced her again. "Actually, I'm returning to London tomorrow." He obviously worked to appear casual. "I have some business to take care of and...you know—"

No. She didn't know. For a split second, she'd actually worried that he would insist on buying her dinner when her stomach rumbled, and she would have to talk her way out of it. Sweet, considerate Rico would have done that. Now, she didn't know what to think. Plus, wasn't he the guy who was in New York so they could get to know each other?

Yes. He was.

Now, suddenly, he was bolting?

Going back to Europe?

It wasn't as if he was just going across town. He was going across an ocean.

Still, in the grand scheme of things, if they were only parents together, nothing more, the reason for his returning to London wasn't any of her business. Technically, they weren't even friends. She had no right to probe.

Sadness filled her but she mustered a smile. "Okay." He was clearly setting boundaries. Which was good—

She supposed.

But hollowness echoed through her. She said the only thing she was allowed to say. "Have a good flight."

He smiled stiffly. "Okay."

He turned and walked down the street, away from her. As he pushed through the crowd, his charcoal gray overcoat began to disappear in fragments until all she saw was a piece of his shoulder and then he was gone.

She swallowed, wondering why she felt so empty when the night before she'd wanted to kick his behind for butting into her business. She turned up the collar on her white wool coat and slid the strap of her big purse up her shoulder and headed down the street.

She told herself she should call a cab, but she wanted the frosty air nipping at her cheeks and appreciated the chance to burn off the energy of everything she was feeling. As Juliette said, they should establish trust, end any thoughts of romance and be friends—

But wouldn't a friend have suggested dinner when her stomach growled?

Something was definitely up with him.

Worse, though, she hated this feeling that now

lived between them. Their relationship had always been fun. Now, it was nothing.

Two weeks later, Rico returned home after a quick trip to Stockholm. Normally, he wouldn't have asked to meet the owner of the company in which he planned to invest, but he'd been nervous and antsy since leaving Marietta on the street that cold night.

She was an adult who'd lived in New York City for years and knew how to navigate the hustle and bustle and even the cold. He hadn't been worried for her safety, especially not in the part of the city of her potential condos.

She also probably had a deli that she frequented for sandwiches or salads when she came home late. All the weird emotions he'd experienced since that night couldn't be concern for her welfare. He trusted her to be smart and take care of herself.

Still, something had bugged him about leaving her that frigid night, and for two weeks he'd paced his downstairs, gone to plays he hadn't wanted to see, visited Antonio and Riley and by extension GiGi, who was over the moon about his baby. Lorenzo hadn't been told to keep it a secret so now a good portion of Italy probably knew he was about to become a dad.

The word was out, and everyone had congratulated him, been happy for him. He was adjusted enough to the idea of becoming a dad that he was happy for himself.

So what the hell was wrong!

He picked up his phone and automatically checked for a text from Marietta, as he'd done a million times in the past two weeks. Because she hadn't reached out to him, he'd assumed she hadn't chosen a condo, but surely by now she had.

Unless she'd changed her mind and decided not to get one of the four that were so perfect—

But wouldn't she have called him?

Actually, he'd told her that she didn't have to. Going with Lorenzo's advice that they should work toward a parents-only relationship, he'd told her she didn't have to call him.

Now, that seemed like a bad idea.

It *was* a bad idea.

And weren't they nearing the time when they could get a DNA test?

Yes. Yes. They were.

So why hadn't she called him?

Because he'd told her not to.

Lorenzo's whole advice wasn't wrong, but maybe Rico had overinterpreted it? Even if he and Marietta only saw each other as parents, they still had to communicate.

He scrolled through his contacts and found her number.

He was calling her. Consequences be damned.

CHAPTER TEN

MARIETTA HALF SAT, half sprawled across the sofa in the living room of the condo she shared with her three friends. They'd been thrilled she was pregnant, sad she was leaving them for her new digs, and now they were out celebrating with their new roommate, a pretty twenty-two-year-old blonde who could have a margarita.

Not that Marietta was upset about not being able to drink alcohol. It was more that her life seemed to change on a dime. Her support systems were crumbling. Her friends wanted different things out of life—

Except Riley. She and Antonio were ready and eager to have kids. She wanted nothing more than to be pregnant at the same time as Marietta.

Unfortunately, she now lived in Florence. Even if she got pregnant tomorrow, they'd have to video call to share the pregnancy experience.

She had a new job.

She was now the boss.

People who had been her work friends were now her staff.

Her life was suddenly so different.

She refused to let herself add Rico into the list of ways her support systems were crumbling, and her life was changing. So, he'd made dividing lines? She respected that. They needed boundaries that would allow them to be together for the sake of their child, but didn't involve intimacy.

Though one would think they should be allowed to communicate. Wouldn't they have to communicate to raise a child?

Of course they would.

Still, Juliette's advice must have been right on some levels. As soon as they'd both pulled back and stopped acting like lovers or even friends, the choice of a condo went smoothly.

She should be glad he wanted nothing to do with her—

Except she missed him. She even missed the guy who forced his way into the decision to buy the condo. Sure. Sure. He was a bit of a nitpicker. But in the end, he'd been right. An elevator was a good idea. So was a second bathroom. And she had gotten a bigger raise than she'd imagined. Adding child support to that, she could afford accommodations that fit having a child.

Her life was great.

Great.

Really great.

No. It wasn't. This whole thing with Rico was off. Wrong. Not that Juliette was wrong. Juliette was never wrong.

Marietta herself simply might have misinterpreted things.

Her phone rang and she bounced up off the sofa, half from surprise and half from eagerness to talk to anyone, rather than sprawl across a piece of furniture trying to sort her changing life.

When she saw the caller was Rico, her heart stopped, then revved up.

She took a minute to calm herself. She would not let him hear relief or eagerness in her voice. Technically, she didn't know this guy. And his behavior had made it clear that he wanted to be involved in their child's life, but not hers.

It was all very logical. Very much what Juliette had also told her. And she had to accept it.

She hit the button to answer the call, calmly saying, "Hello, Rico."

"Hello, Miss Boots-in-the-Oven-but-That-Don't-Make-'em-Biscuits."

She laughed. "If you can't appreciate a good ol' Southern explanation of truth, you're missing out on a lot of fun in life."

"I'm definitely missing out on a lot of fun in life. Your condo for one. I don't even know if you got one. How you're feeling for another. And if you've seen a doctor yet. And just plain you. Apparently, I like hearing about boots and ovens."

She laughed, but happy tears sprang to her eyes. "I like telling you about boots and ovens."

She sat back on the sofa, enjoying the shuffle of relief that softened her muscles and calmed her nerves.

"So how are you?"

"Good. No problems so far. And, yes, I did see a doctor and, yes, I'm pregnant. For honest to God real now."

"You're telling me I should see my lawyer and set up child support payments?"

"Do you want me to get the DNA test first?"

For a few seconds he didn't say anything. "Honestly, I believe you when you say the baby is mine. One of the first things you told me after we made love was that it had been a while for you."

"I coulda been talking about two weeks."

He laughed. "You were too eager. Either that or I swept you off your feet."

"Oh, you swept."

He laughed again and everything inside her bubbled with joy. This was what they needed to do. Communicate. Not avoid each other. She wouldn't forget Juliette's advice about keeping some distance. She would simply modify it.

"What have you been doing?"

His voice became businesslike. "Wheeling and dealing."

"Buy anything good?"

"I'm investing in a corporation that's working on establishing a crypto currency system."

"Isn't there already one?"

"Sort of. We're searching for a way to keep everyone honest. Something like the New York Stock Exchange, but for crypto. How about you? Did you buy a condo?"

"We're in escrow. We should close in two weeks."

"Which one did you get?"

"The first one we saw on the second night."

"I liked that one."

"So did I. Now I'm thinking about getting a cat."

Rico sat up on his sofa. "A cat? You're about to have a child! What do you want with a cat?"

"Pets are very good for children. Plus, I always had a cat back home in Texas. Had to leave Sophia Maria Lolita Conchita Chequita Banana behind when I left for New York. Didn't let my ex have her though. My mom took her in. We video called once a week until she passed."

She paused and he heard her suck in a breath, as if she was preventing herself from crying.

He swallowed hard. For as funny as she tried to make the story, he could feel the love she had for her pet and understand that she missed her. All the same, he kept the mood light.

"That's a lotta names for a something that probably didn't weigh twenty pounds. Was she named after relatives?"

"No. She just showed up at our door one day, so we didn't know her family. But she was a big personality. Too many good things about her for her to have only one name."

"She sounds like fun."

"She was. She was a warrior princess who kept the rodents away. Not just for our property, but the neighbors' too. That's why I want another cat."

He winced. "For rodent control?"

She laughed. "No! For company. But I need a cat who's not accustomed to being outside."

"Okay, but any cat isn't going to like being stuck in your condo all the time. If you chose a dog for a pet, you could walk it."

"I can get my new cat a leash and walk her too."

He laughed. "I would pay to see that."

"Well, you could come out to see that once I get settled."

He missed her enough that he wasn't sure he could wait that long. "How about if I come out and help you move?"

"There's not much to move. Our furniture was shared and there's an unwritten rule that if a roommate leaves, they kiss the furniture good-bye. I'm even leaving my big closet-like cabinet."

"Okay. How about this? What if I come out and help you celebrate your new home? We can go out to dinner or see a show."

There was a pause. A long one. Eventually, she said, "You mean like a date?"

The concept flummoxed him for a second. He'd never taken the mother of his child on a date. And now, he wasn't supposed to. There were lines that couldn't be crossed.

But he'd missed her. And it didn't seem right to have a child with someone and treat them like…

He wasn't sure what Lorenzo's "neutrality" meant. How could he treat this woman who was giving him a child like…nothing?

Screw it.

"Yes. Like a date."

"Really?"

"What? You don't like me?"

"I like you fine. It's just that…"

"You think there are lines we shouldn't cross?"

"Yes."

Everything began to fall into place in his head. Her talking to Juliette. Him talking to Lorenzo.

"Because of something Juliette said to you?"

She paused long enough to confirm his suspicion. But she sighed and said, "Rico, this is about more than Juliette's advice. A child binds us. We will be going to birthday parties and dance recitals and graduations and planning a wedding for this baby when the time comes."

"And?"

"And I love all that. But I want all those times we're together to be cordial. Which means there probably shouldn't be anything more between us. We had a fling. We like each other enough that we could have probably kept that fling going for a while. But things end. Even marriages that start out good can end. I know things about marriage that you don't know—"

"I never asked you to marry me."

"I know. But while Antonio and Riley have an innocence that will carry them through a long happy life and Lorenzo and Juliette are so perfectly suited they'll complement each other forever. You and I are neither innocent nor Legos."

"Legos?"

"The little blocks that fit together."

"I know what they are. I just don't think anybody wants to be described as a block."

She sighed. "And I don't want to get into another bad relationship. Or ruin what we have. Our child has to come first."

"Agreed. But if we both don't believe in fairy tales," he said, even though the Cinderella comparison kept slapping him in the face because right now he felt like one of the stepsisters who didn't fit into the shoe, "maybe we could have something better."

He could hear the skepticism in her voice when she said, "Something better?"

"Trust?"

"Trust?"

Things Lorenzo said began to piece together in

his head. "My parents, the people I should have been able to trust, didn't want me. I grew up in a system that I only trusted enough to acknowledge that everyone was *trying* to do their best for me. The first chance I got I bailed, believing I could take better care of myself than the government could. I trusted myself. And when your marriage ended and you moved to New York City, you trusted yourself."

"I did."

"Because you've been hurt. And I've been hurt. And we know life's not easy. Trust is more important than anything else. So what if we trusted each other?"

"To do what exactly?"

"To be honest. To admit it when whatever romance we have is over and let each other go without anger. To do the best we each can do for our child."

"That's an interesting concept. It sounds like the opposite of marriage vows. Rather than the promise to stay together, you're proposing we promise to let each other go peacefully."

In spite of the negativity of her reasoning, he knew she got the concept. "It's how I've lived my life. I trust someone or a situation until the trust is breached. Then I walk away. But I don't walk away angry."

"You shake the dust from your feet and start over? No hard feelings?"

"Yes. No hard feelings. If we both promise to be honest, both promise that neither one of us will cheat or stay in the relationship past the life of our feelings—"

"Then we can be romantic?"

"Yes. For as long as it lasts."

"It's about trust?"

"And honesty. Do you think we could do that?"

She didn't really know what she thought. What he'd said seemed too good to be true. But she supposed if there was one thing she could promise him it would be honesty.

After all, what choice did she have? They would be together in some way, shape or form for at least eighteen years. They had to get along and they also needed to figure out what to do with their attraction. Maybe letting it run its course before the baby was born would be the end of it?

"Okay. We'll try your way."

They talked for another twenty minutes about her condo and his insistence that he should be there to help her set up her home. She couldn't talk him out of it, so she knew he'd be arriving the weekend she took possession of her new place. The condo would have no furniture. She'd planned on buying a sleeping bag and sleeping on the floor until she got everything set up.

Just for the heck of it, she decided to buy a second sleeping bag to tease him. She knew he'd probably get a room at a fancy hotel while he was in Manhattan, but it would be funny to make him think she expected him to sleep on the floor.

The following evening, Marietta left the office sliding into her white wool coat. She buttoned it in the elevator and said good-night to Fred the doorman as she walked through the lobby to the street.

The temperature felt as if it'd dropped a million degrees. With a deep breath, she joined the crowd of commuters heading toward the subway entrance. But she didn't get four feet before someone fell in step with her.

"Hey."

His accent sent shivers through her blood. She stopped. "Rico?"

"I said I missed you."

She laughed. "Oh, you billionaires. Drop one hint and you land on our doorstep."

He eased her out of the crowd, to the entryway for another building, pulled her to him and kissed her. She let herself fall into the delicious kiss, the warmth, the passion, all the while thinking of the weird promise they'd made to each other.

She hated to look at this wonderful kiss as step one of letting their attraction run its course, but considering this little fling of theirs to be anything other than temporary was ridiculous. Plus, if they really wanted to have a solid friendship as they raised their child, it was smart to get the sexual attraction out of their systems.

He pulled back. "There. I feel better now."

She allowed the little jolt of happiness that formed to ripple though her. "I suppose I missed you too."

He slid his arm across her shoulders and led her onto the street again. "Just what a guy wants to hear." He stopped in front of a big, black SUV. "I rented a car."

She eyed it skeptically. "Looks like a minibus."

"It could easily get us to your apartment where you could pack a few things for tonight and work tomorrow morning…maybe tomorrow night and work the next day—"

She gaped at him. "How long are you staying?"

"I can only stay two days. Well, two nights. Plus, I promised you a date and things will be too rushed tonight. It would probably be better to get Chinese food delivered to my hotel room."

"I could eat Chinese."

He opened the SUV door. "Good. Punch your address into the GPS and we'll get this party started."

She smiled as he closed the door behind her, but as he rounded the SUV's hood, she prayed they were doing the right thing.

She didn't want to get her heart broken, or break his, but there was no future for them. She had to keep reminding herself of that.

Because if anybody could tempt her into falling in love it would be Rico. She had to be smart, keep a little distance, guard her heart. Or she'd ruin everything. Not just their parenting together, but the life and confidence she'd built after her disastrous marriage.

She could never go back.

CHAPTER ELEVEN

HIS ROOM TURNED out to be the penthouse suite of one of the best hotels in the city. Because they ordered their Chinese food in the car on the drive from her apartment to his hotel, it was waiting for them in the kitchen area of his room.

Walking inside, he shrugged out of his overcoat. He tossed it on the back of a white sofa and used a remote to bring the fireplace to life. "It's cold out there. The fire makes it cozy."

"Yeah. Cozy." Pulling her small wheeled suitcase behind her, she looked around. This was very different from the cute hotel they'd stayed at in Florence. Very different. "Wow."

"I usually stay in this suite when I'm here for business." He pointed to their left. "There's a conference room back there." He pointed at the small area with a refrigerator, stove, microwave, dishwasher and sink. "A little kitchenette. A huge bedroom suite." He huffed out a breath. "It's very convenient."

Convenient?

It was huge. And gorgeous.

"Convenient for doing business?"

He walked over and pulled her to him. The move was so natural she didn't have time to think, only react by melting against him.

"For doing anything I want." He kissed her quickly. "But right now I'm starving. So let's eat."

A little dazzled, she stepped away from him. "Let me take my bag to the room."

"Okay, you do that. I'll dish the food. I'm warning you though, if there's an extra egg roll, it's mine."

She laughed and headed to the double doors at the end of a short corridor. She opened them on an exquisite bedroom. Lush with the textures of silks, weaves and wood in lamps, chairs and bedside tables, the simple beige-and-white room took her breath away.

She slipped out of her coat and hung it in a closet before hanging her two work outfits beside it. She put her makeup in the bathroom, telling herself she wasn't stalling—just in awe. It was the first time since she met Rico that she saw his wealth. Sure, she could have seen it in the Bentley, but lots of people had nice cars. He dressed well, but usually casually. Though he wore a white shirt and tie today, he'd covered them with a leather jacket. Not a suit coat.

She'd never seen how he lived.

She glanced around. She'd bet his house in

London was a lot like this. Which was why he was so comfortable here and why she was taking everything in, touching silky lampshades and shiny wood surfaces.

Yet another reason it was a good thing their romance had a shelf life. She did not belong in this world and even with her new condo he'd be slumming any time he visited her.

Needing to relax, she took off her work clothes and slipped into sweatpants and a big T-shirt.

When she arrived in the kitchenette, where he sat on a tall chair beside the island that acted as a table, he laughed.

"I wanted you to get comfy, but now I feel overdressed."

"Yeah." But he looked great. Leather jacket off. Sleeves of his white shirt rolled to his elbows. Tie loosened.

It didn't matter what he wore or how he wore it, he managed to look sexy and yummy.

She slid onto the chair beside his and dug into her chicken fried rice with a groan of contentment. "I didn't realize how hungry I was."

"What did you have for lunch?"

"Salad."

He grimaced. "You might have to add a sandwich to that while you're pregnant."

She peered over at him. "How would you know?"

"I've been reading up on pregnancy."

"Oh." She wasn't sure if that was good or bad but remembering what Juliette had said about how he would want to be a part of his child's life, she understood.

"In addition to gaining weight, your feet are going to swell. Your back will hurt. And don't even get me started on bladder control."

She shook her head. "Such a sweet talker."

"And this whole time nothing will happen to me."

"Humph. It would be interesting if something did happen to fathers. You know, a guy couldn't deny paternity if he threw up every time his pregnant girlfriend did."

He laughed. "Yeah. Evolution wasn't really fair about that." He paused. "Though if you think about it, fathers might have been created to miss out on trouble so they could ward off predators and hunt for food."

"I suppose it all goes back to caveman days. I'm glad we've evolved past that, and I can earn my own living, make my own way."

His expression changed. He almost looked disappointed, but he said, "I'd like to think I would be handy with predators."

"How are you with a crossbow?"

He laughed. "Yes. Your point is taken. We have evolved and I am useless."

She didn't want to insult him or leave him out.

They were supposed to be establishing trust. "You're not useless!"

"Really?"

"Hey, I agreed to child support. I took your advice about a building with an elevator. I even understand your stance on enjoying our romance while it lasts and moving on."

"Meaning, I'm your idea man?"

"Yes." She took advantage of the silence that followed to dig into her chicken, but she suddenly wondered about his parents. She knew his difficult start in life was what dictated his reactions now. He wouldn't leave his child to fend for itself—or with only a mom. He would be a part of this. He wouldn't just take responsibility. He wanted to help raise this baby.

"Do you ever wonder about your parents?"

"I used to." He lifted his dish from the center island, rinsed it and put it in the dishwasher. "But when I was about seven, I realized there wasn't much point in trying to guess who they might have been or why they didn't want me, and I stopped."

"That's too bad because there are a lot of angles a seven-year-old kid might not have explored. For instance, what if it wasn't your mom who left you but your grandmother?"

He gaped at her. "How is that better?"

"I'm not looking for *better*. I'm looking for alternative origin stories. Being left in that train station might have been the best thing that could have happened for you."

He crossed his arms on his chest. "This I've gotta hear."

She would have laughed at the skepticism in his voice, but this was important, serious. "What if your parents had died and your grandmother couldn't support you? What if she was trying to give you a better life? Or what if your mother was the one to leave you and she did it to protect you from an abusive dad."

His face changed, softened. "That would have been awful for her."

"Yes. Or you could be the heir to the throne in a country that overthrew its monarchy, and all royals were executed."

His lips twitched with the effort not to laugh.

"Okay, maybe not a monarchy but a crime family. What if your mom wanted something better for you than the vicious cycle of that kind of life? Then she wouldn't merely have saved you, but also your child..." She pointed at her stomach. "*This* child...would have been born into that life if she hadn't gotten you out."

He uncrossed his arms and studied her for a few seconds. "A seven-year-old is definitely too young to consider things like that."

"There might not be a million reasons why a mother would believe she was protecting her child by letting him go, but there are a just enough for you to realize you might have been loved so much, that your mom believed she had to take you out of your circumstance to save you."

He looked stunned, as if unable to take it all in. "That's amazing to consider."

"You always believed you weren't wanted. But what if you were loved so much your mom made the ultimate sacrifice."

He rubbed his hands down his face. "You're asking me to shift my entire life's beliefs."

"It's not your entire life. Your work won't change. Your friendships won't change. Considering a different reason your mom left you only broadens your horizons a bit. It's not like you're going from an armadillo to a turtle. You're simply considering that maybe you shouldn't believe the worst about your beginnings. After all, not knowing for sure and not being able to know for sure, means you can believe the best if you want."

He sucked in a breath. "That's a bigger shift than you think it is."

"Hey. You should be pregnant." She tossed her napkin on her now empty plate. "It feels like my life changed completely in the time it took to snap my fingers."

He snorted, but raised his gaze to the ceiling, then brought it back to her. "Is this your way of telling me I'm asking a lot of you?"

"By having our baby? No! I want this child! I can't wait to be a mom. And I'm happy to do the shifting. I'm just saying some of the hardest shifts are the ones we're forced to make. Or the ones we *need* to make when circumstances change."

He thought about that. "You're saying that I've focused for so long on the bad reasons someone would abandon me and never considered that I might not have been abandoned but rescued."

"Like Moses in the basket."

He walked over and sat beside her. "You might think I don't know that story, but I do."

"Of course you do." She leaned in and gave him a quick kiss. "In order to make good investments, you study. Probably a lot. It makes you a well-rounded person and that might be another gift your mother gave you."

"Being well rounded? You think having to learn everything on my own made me well-rounded?"

"I know a lot of people who went to university, but they didn't really learn practical applications. Your entire life is practical applications. I would bet you could do anything you want."

She tried to shift away, but he caught her shoulders and kept her right where she was. He gazed into her eyes as if mesmerized, then he kissed her, long and deep. The emotion of it tripped something in her heart, but she caught it before it could fully kick in.

She knew the kiss was an expression of his appreciation of her take on his life and she stood by it. With her own child growing in her belly, she could clearly see the lengths she would go to protect a baby she hadn't even met yet. The love that radiated through her filled her with strength and resolve.

That's the feeling she got when she pondered Rico's mom leaving him. Strength and resolve and a protectiveness she'd never felt before.

That was also why she'd never take away his right to be part of his child's life. Maybe this baby was his opportunity to experience emotion so strong that he could finally come to terms with his own beginnings?

He broke the kiss but barely moved away from her, whispering, "Wanna go back and see the bedroom suite?"

She laughed. "I already saw it."

"I have new things to show you."

She didn't doubt it for a second.

He kissed her again, easing her off her stool to stand. She let herself enjoy the feeling of him as she slid her arms up his forearms to his biceps and the sensation of pressing against him when she moved in to deepen their kiss.

She'd never felt this way with anyone. While she knew that might be because she'd begun dating her ex when she was young, she wouldn't downplay all the wonderful sensations and even the closeness she felt with a guy she barely knew.

CHAPTER TWELVE

THEY KISSED THEIR way back to his room, then, like an old married couple, they broke apart to remove shirts and pants. They could have come together in a storm of passion. Everything about her made him hot and hungry. And happy. But he knew about the temporary nature of life. Even her possible origin story of his mother protecting him proved that moving on was a part of life. She had a bad marriage and wouldn't risk her sanity again. He didn't have to get married to know that the best way to move through life was unencumbered. Ultimately, they would drift apart. But tonight, she was his and he intended to enjoy that.

They rolled across the bed, kissing and touching, then she began the tasting. He loved the feel of her tongue as it slid across his chest, down his belly. But he'd missed her so much in the past few weeks, that the pleasure pain intensified to the point that he had to stop her. He caught her shoulder and rolled her to her back, joining them and taking the sensations to the next level until they both cascaded over the edge of reason with a groan of delight.

He fell asleep holding her. Content in a way he'd never felt before. But, better, when he woke up, she was still there. In his bed.

The most wonderful emotion fluttered through him. He watched her sleep for a few minutes, then remembered how she'd been starving the night before and went to the kitchen to make her breakfast.

When the eggs, toast and bacon were ready, she ambled out and stood by the center island. Fully dressed. She probably thought she could race out the door, but she'd clearly underestimated the power of crispy bacon.

He answered the questions in her eyes when she glanced at the food on the center island. "Every other time we've been together, you've ditched me."

"Ditched you?"

"Maybe that's a little too negative. But I always woke alone. Today, I did not. So, I thought I'd surprise you with breakfast, give you a reason to always want to stay the night."

She eased her way to one of the stools. "For a man of the world, you don't seem to understand the simple realities of normal people with jobs."

He motioned for her to take a seat. She set her purse on the chair beside her, and he slid breakfast in front of her.

"I have time for the eggs, but I'll take the bacon and coffee to go."

"Yes, ma'am." He wrapped some bacon for her and poured coffee into one of the paper cups supplied by the hotel for busy businesspeople who would be jetting off to meetings and taking their morning coffee with them.

She ate the eggs and toast so quickly he wasn't sure if she was late or starving, but either way, he'd fed her, made sure she didn't leave the house hungry.

Pride swelled in his chest.

When she rushed out for work, the penthouse suite echoed with quiet, but it was good quiet. Still, after an hour of researching prospective investments on his laptop, he got antsy.

He picked up his phone and texted his mentor, Ethan O'Banyon, asking if he wanted to meet for lunch. Within seconds, he got a return text suggesting a restaurant. Two hours later they were sitting in a quiet dining room with white linen tablecloths and waiters in dark trousers and white shirts.

Ethan ordered a martini. The waiter scampered away.

Rico said, "So, how's retirement?"

"What retirement?" Ethan, a short balding man, who still looked like a tycoon in a suit and tie, laughed. "You know people like us don't retire."

Rico shook his head. "I guess not. But I would

like to think that by then I'll be putting the bulk of my money into something safe, something I don't have to watch as much."

"Oh, now where's the fun in that?"

Rico laughed. "I have to think a little more responsibly now. I'm about to have a child."

Ethan's face filled with joy. "Rico! And you let me order a martini when we should be drinking champagne?"

"Eh. You wasted a couple of bucks." He hailed the waiter. "Get us a bottle of champagne."

The waiter nodded and left.

Ethan sucked in a long breath. "I cannot believe you're having a child."

"Technically, my..." He fumbled over what to call Marietta. She was too interesting and he liked her too much for her to be something as pedestrian as a girlfriend. "My baby's mother is having the child."

"You're not married?" He paused. "Of course you're not. You would have invited me to the wedding. So what's up with this?"

"Neither of us believes in marriage. In fact, we're doing the opposite. To stay on good terms for the sake of our baby, we've promised to split amicably when the romance dies."

Ethan just stared at him. "What?"

"We don't want to mess up our kid's life with our bad behavior, so we're ending things before they get ugly in order to stay friends."

Ethan continued to stare at him. Then he shook his head as if trying to think it through and failing. Ethan was older. His values and views on some things were dated. Rico never questioned him about his choices or beliefs. He respected him. And Ethan never pushed Rico into things that weren't right for him.

The champagne came. The waiter opened it and poured two glasses. As the young man walked away, Ethan raised his glass. "Congratulations."

They touched glasses. Rico said, "Thanks."

"With the exception of the romance being a bit off, you seem happy."

"I am happy."

"Then I am happy for you," Ethan said. "So what's she like?"

Rico said, "Funny. Interesting." He laughed. "She's from Texas and has an odd way of looking at life."

"Ah, Texas. Cattle. Oil. Money. The money almost got me to settle there myself, but I like city life."

"I do too."

Ethan took a sip of his champagne and set his glass on the table. "So, you like her because she's different?"

"She's not different. She has a different take on things that sort of fascinates me. Last night, she suggested that I flip my beliefs about who left me at that train station and why."

Ethan's face contorted. "Flip it to what?"

"Instead of thinking my mom left me because she didn't want me, Marietta suggest that I consider that my father was abusive, or a career criminal, and my mom was trying to get me out of that life."

Looking oddly relieved, Ethan pulled in a breath and picked up his champagne glass. "You'll never know."

"That's what I thought! It's pointless to think about it. But I could tell that's not how she feels. She called whatever I believe about why I was abandoned my 'origin story.'"

Ethan laughed. "Like a comic book hero?"

"I don't know."

The waiter returned and they ordered lunch. Their conversation turned to some upcoming investment possibilities Ethan wanted Rico's opinion on and Rico suddenly realized that their roles had reversed. Rico had always been the one asking for Ethan's opinion. Now, Ethan didn't merely trust Rico. He depended on him.

They finished lunch and walked out into the sunny—but cold—February day.

"I'm thrilled about your child," Ethan said, hugging Rico. "But I want you to promise me one thing."

"Sure. If I can."

"Keep an open mind."

"About?"

"About life."

"I've always had an open mind about life."

Ethan made the odd face again. "Yes and no. I just don't want you to ruin the experience of having a child because you're hung up on other stuff."

"You mean my origin story."

Ethan shook his head. "Yes. Forget all that. Focus on your child. Or maybe focus on your baby's mom. She sounds lovely. Like somebody you might want to keep around for a while."

"Ethan, we'll be in each other's life for years... decades."

"Yes, well, it sounds like she's more to you than the mother of your child. Thinking about things like that silly origin story might keep you from seeing that. Love is a surprising thing. Not always what we think it is."

"We're not going to fall in love. Neither one of us wants that."

"Whatever."

Rico smiled at Ethan's sarcastic, "Whatever," before the old man said, "Goodbye," and walked away.

Rico watched him go. He'd already promised Marietta that they would let their relationship dissolve when it was over. And that's what he intended to do. After all, that had been *his* idea.

But packing his things to return to London the following morning after Marietta left for work, Ethan's words popped up in his brain again.

Love is a surprising thing. Not always what we think it is.

He batted his hand in dismissal. He'd already made his decisions and if the two days he'd just spent with Marietta were any indicator, he'd made a good choice. They'd had fun. They always had fun. If they handled their relationship correctly, being a parent with her would also be fun. He did not want to risk their good relationship on something as fleeting as love.

He knew from experience that love did not last. And if he ever thought it did, all he had to do was remember being left in a train station—

Except, what if what Marietta said was true? What if he hadn't been abandoned but rescued, saved from something like an abusive home or a life that was more of a prison than a life?

Then he hadn't been left at a train station out of selfishness. He'd been left out of love.

Real love.

The possibility nearly floored him.

He drove his SUV to the airport and tossed his keys to an employee with instructions to return it to the car rental office, then he climbed aboard his private jet.

But as he walked into the cabin, he looked around with fresh eyes.

Would he even have any of this if his mother hadn't loved him enough to rescue him?

* * *

Feeling silly happy, Marietta ordered two sleeping bags, which were delivered the Thursday before she took possession of her condo. Friday night, Jake the videographer and Layla the new photographer helped her cart her boxes of clothes from her apartment to a car she'd rented.

At the condo, as if they'd been given instructions from Juliette not to let her lift anything, Layla put all her boxes on a bellboy's cart and Jake held a sleeping bag under each arm as they rode the elevator to her floor.

She unlocked the door and presented her new home to her friends. The open floor plan. The white kitchen. The fireplace. The view from huge sliding glass doors on the wall in front of the terrace.

Layla said, "Oh, my goodness!" She spun to face Marietta. "It's gorgeous!"

Jake shrugged, saying, "It's nice." High praise from a guy who didn't talk a lot.

Marietta laughed. "It's perfect for me and a baby. That's what counts."

Jake rolled the bellboy's cart down the hall to the main bedroom and Layla began ripping the packaging off the first sleeping bag.

Marietta stopped her. "It's fine. I can do that."

Layla held the sleeping bag away from her. "You have eight boxes to unpack once we're gone. Let me unwrap this."

"Okay. Fine." She glanced around. "I don't even have water to offer you."

Unraveling the long strand of plastic around the sleeping bag, Layla said, "Then why don't you run down to the convenience store and get a few things, while I unwrap these and Jake unloads the cart in the bedroom."

"That might not be a bad idea."

"Or maybe you don't need to." Rico walked in the door they'd left open. He held out two bags. "I got bottled water. Some bagels and cream cheese for morning." He walked over and kissed Marietta. "And wine."

Layla stared at them. Her eyes round and curious.

Marietta laughed. "This is Rico. Baby's dad."

Layla's eyes lit. "*This* is Rico?"

He pointed at his chest. "Baby's dad."

"You know you're going to have to drink that wine out of the bottle because I don't even have glasses."

He shrugged out of his overcoat. "That's fine. You weren't getting any anyway." He looked around. "So…no furniture. Probably no bedding."

She winced. "I do have towels. And sleeping bags." She grinned at him. "I've got to warn you. If you're going back to your fancy hotel, you're going alone."

He glanced at the sleeping bag Layla was unwrapping and then at Marietta. "You can't sleep on the floor."

"Of course I can. This is my first night in my new home. I want to experience it. Sleeping bags and all."

He groaned and shook his head.

Marietta said, "Go help Jake unload the boxes in the bedroom so Layla and Jake can go home. I appreciate their help getting my boxes here, but I don't want to keep them all night."

Rico walked back through the hall to the bedroom and Marietta and Layla unwrapped the two sleeping bags and unrolled them.

"Let's put them in front of the fireplace."

Layla laughed. "Are you really going to make that good-looking guy sleep on the floor?"

"Hey, this is my first night as a homeowner. If he wants to be part of the experience, then he's sleeping on the floor."

They laid out the sleeping bags. As they finished, Jake and Rico walked up the hall.

Jake said, "Everything that can be done is done. Boxes are off the cart. Technically, you need to go through them to see where to store things. Though it's not like you have a dresser. Just a closet."

"Doesn't matter. It's all clothes," Marietta said. "I have to go online tomorrow and order things like glasses and dishes."

"Or we could take the SUV to a shopping center." Rico pulled out his phone. "There's got to be one around here somewhere."

Layla said, "Maybe Jersey."

Marietta frowned. "New Jersey? Go the whole way to New Jersey for dishes?"

"And sheets and towels and furniture."

"I'm with Marietta. Just shop online," Jake said, walking into the living space to peek at the fireplace. "You'll pay for delivery, but it's worth it to have somebody else have to cart your sofa into the service elevator and get it up here."

Rico said, "Maybe we start online and go to brick-and-mortar stores for things we can't find."

Layla lifted her coat from the center island. The only flat surface in the apartment to store anything. "Makes sense." She hugged Marietta. "I'll see you on Monday."

Jake waved. "See you on Monday."

And then they were gone. Closing the door behind them, they left Marietta and Rico alone in the echoing condo.

Rico said, "I love it. You did a good job choosing a home."

She glanced around proudly. "I did."

His gaze collided with the sleeping bags in front of the fireplace. "So, you're really going to make me sleep on the floor?"

"Yes."

"Marietta, there's nothing here. Not even a television to amuse us. Let's go back to my hotel."

She walked over and began unbuttoning his shirt. "I can think of something to amuse us."

He laughed. "There is that." He frowned. "Except I have an idea." He knelt down before the first sleeping bag. "Let's see if this works." He unzipped it and spread it out. Then he tugged the second sleeping bag over and unzipped it. He laid it on top of the first one like a blanket.

"Oh, so we can cuddle."

"Now, wait. I'm not done." He found the zipper for the first bag and then the second, fusing them together.

She laughed. "You're making one big sleeping bag."

"The events of my childhood did give me some interesting skills."

"Well, this one looks like fun. But there's one more thing." She raced into the kitchen, opened drawers until she found what she wanted and pulled out one of the many manufacturers' instruction sheets for the appliances. She rifled through them until she found the one for the fireplace. "Here it is."

She ambled back to Rico, reading the instructions, then hit the button that brought the flames to life. She smiled at Rico. "It's gas."

"That's handy." Then he patted the sleeping bag.

She smiled and knelt beside him. Crazy feelings bombarded her, mostly tingles of arousal.

But also great joy. She had a home now. Soon she'd have a baby. And she liked her baby's dad.

She couldn't remember ever being this happy. He kissed her and for sure she knew she'd never been this happy. Bubbly. Content.

But relationships were temporary. Not permanent. Her baby and her new home had to be what filled her with joy. Rico might be part of it but she'd been in a marriage. She'd watched love fizzle, then die, then turn into something awful.

She would never again go that route. She'd enjoy him while he was with her, but when the baby came she would insist they focus their attention on being good parents.

CHAPTER THIRTEEN

RICO SLEPT BETTER than he had in years. The fireplace was warm, but so was the sleeping bag, especially when he was snuggled against Marietta. Without opening his eyes, he reached for her, but she was gone. The condo smelled different too.

Hearing her in the kitchen, he said, "What are you doing?"

"I put the bagels you bought in the oven."

Still not opening his eyes, he mumbled, "But that don't make 'em biscuits."

"Hold that thought," she said, her voice moving away.

He groaned. "What now? I've already slept on a floor in front of a fire. That's all the down-home stuff I want to do this weekend. If there's no bed here by six o'clock tonight, we sleep in my hotel room."

The sound of her moving around in the kitchen echoed in the open space. "Or we could sleep in my mom's guest room."

He bolted up, positive he hadn't heard right. "What?"

"My mom called this morning. The condo impressed her, but she might have—actually, she totally did—seen you sleeping in front of the fireplace."

His eyes bugged. "Your mother saw me?" His eyes widened even farther. "I'm naked!"

"You were covered. She saw nothing…just that there was a man sleeping in my condo…" She winced. "With me."

"Damn it."

"Haven't you ever been caught with a woman?" She laughed. "You're in your thirties. You're an adult. You're the sexiest man alive. People know you're not celibate."

He ran his hand down his face. She handed him a toasted bagel, slathered in cream cheese.

"Oven toasted. I have my unusual skills too."

Too hungry to be picky, he bit into it and groaned. "Okay. That's delicious."

"Anyway, go back to your hotel and pack a bag. My mother wants to meet you."

"Today?" he asked incredulously. "You want to go to Texas today?"

"Today is as good of a day as any because… I also told them I'm pregnant and they're curious about you. And I want you to go so my parents can see you're a normal, nice guy."

Horrified, he glanced around. "Okay, remember how we said we'd build our relationship on trust and honesty?"

"Yeah."

"Well, I'm going to be honest and say I'm not ready to meet them. And meeting them also shouldn't be spur-of-the-moment. Let's plan a weekend to go. That will give me a chance to pack appropriately and your parents time to adjust to us being pregnant."

She frowned. "I guess."

"I *know* and we are sleeping in the hotel tonight." He slid out of the sleeping bag. "But first, get your computer. We have some shopping to do."

"Okay, but really there's nothing for you to worry about meeting my parents. My mom is cool. My dad's even cooler. You're going to love them."

Hundreds of reasons that couldn't be true filled his brain. He was an orphan. A confirmed bachelor. He'd gotten their daughter pregnant. He made a point of never meeting anybody's parents. But he supposed this situation was different. Partially because Marietta believed she couldn't have children. Maybe the baby was a point in his favor? And maybe by the time they actually went to Texas all of that would have sunk in for them?

He hoped.

But for now, they were staying in her condo and there was shopping to do.

* * *

Slowly but surely, furniture began to arrive in Marietta's new home. Even though Rico flew to Manhattan every Friday night to watch her condo take shape, she spent those two weeks doing Valentine-themed proposals and he spent Saturdays and Sundays alone.

But that also meant they couldn't go to Texas until the first weekend in March. Which really did give him time to adjust to the idea of meeting her parents.

They slept in her new bed that Friday night and woke Saturday morning for the flight to Texas. Everything went smoothly and a few hours later, he was driving a rental car up a small incline when her family home came into view. The brown brick one-story house seemed to stretch forever.

Though he'd been calm the whole time, the hair on the back of his neck suddenly began to prickle. He had never been in the situation of meeting the parents of the woman who would be having his child. It all seemed so normal in Italy, London or Manhattan where people were sophisticated and suave. But here—in the country, the home of cowboys and hardworking folk—he wasn't so sure anymore.

They drove down a long lane to the house. Rico glanced around. Just as with the Salvaggio vineyard, there was nothing for miles except green grass and fences surrounding outbuildings. One was clearly a big barn.

He got out of the SUV they'd rented at the airport, looking around. "Your parents own all this?"

"It's a ranch."

He knew that. "I just hadn't expected it to be so big or so green. And where are the cattle?"

She laughed, making her curls shimmy as she got out of the SUV. "It might not be what you pictured in your mind, but you're going to love it here. Trust me." As soon as her car door closed, she said, "When we get to the house, let me do the talking."

"Protecting me?"

"No. I just know how to make my dad see that me having a baby is a dream come true."

"Should I be worried?"

"I'm a grown woman who has lived away from home for five years. My parents don't get a say in how I live my life." She winced. "But my dad will react."

She headed up a stone path toward the front door.

He gaped at the space she left behind, then he raced after her. "Your dad will *react*?"

She reached the door. "This *is* Texas. And I'm his baby girl. He's going to…have some thoughts on that. And he's probably going to tell you all of them."

"And you never told me this because…?"

She shrugged. "It never came up. Besides, he'll be fine once he gets it all out. I told you he's cool." She waited for him before opening the house door. "Come on. It's not going to be bad. And you'll like my family. Actually, I think you'll love my two brothers."

They stepped into a foyer that was open to the general living space. He could see shiny white tile floors in a cream-and-beige living room and dining room and an all-white kitchen.

As she walked toward the kitchen, she called, "We're here."

But she hadn't needed to. Everybody seemed to have congregated around a big center island with gray, black and white granite counter tops. His gaze swept the room, then stopped on Juliette and Lorenzo.

Juliette and Lorenzo?

As Marietta hugged and was hugged, he walked up to Lorenzo. "What are you doing here?"

Juliette laughed. "Cole's roasting a pig. They called earlier in the week, said it would be fun for us to jet on down since you and Marietta were going to be here. What took you so long to get here?"

Rico wanted to say, how do you know the Fontains? But he didn't get the chance. A big guy in a cowboy hat opened the sliding glass doors and entered. "Going to be hot for March."

Marietta seemed to take that as her cue. She

caught Rico's arm and turned him toward the guy in the cowboy hat and a red-haired waif who Rico assumed was her mom.

"Mom, Dad, this is Rico."

The waif threw herself at him and hugged him. The big guy gave him the once-over.

Adding the hug to the way everyone was in jeans and a T-shirt, even Lorenzo, Rico suddenly felt overdressed and totally out of place.

Still, as a former foster child, he wasn't a stranger to being the odd man out. As Marietta's mom released him, he approached the big guy with his hand extended. "It's a pleasure to meet you."

Her dad still eyed him suspiciously. "That's what everyone says."

Marietta beamed with joy. "My dad's really well loved in the community." She hooked her arm with his, clearly proud of him. "He's head of the cattleman's association."

Her dad finally took Rico's extended hand and shook it. "Have been for thirty years."

He suddenly realized that the eyes of ten strangers were on him. Two guys. Could be her brothers. Two women. Could be her brothers' wives. Six kids.

Six kids?

Marietta pointed to the first man. "That's Danny and his wife, Tonya, and their four kids."

Rico shook Danny's hand. The kids waved shyly.

"That's Junior," she said, pointing at the second brother, "his wife, Cindy Lou, and their two daughters."

One of the daughters hid behind her mother.

Discomfort crept up on him. Not because they were staring at him but because he suddenly realized how odd he must look to them in his chinos and golf shirt.

Plus, to them he probably spoke weirdly.

And he was the father of Marietta's child.

A child everybody believed she couldn't have.

Sheesh. He might as well be from Mars because to these people he was an alien.

The kitchen began to fill with conversation and laughter. Marietta's mom, Sheila, told him to get their bags while Marietta caught up with everyone.

Grateful, he left the noisy kitchen, brought their overnight bags into the house and met Sheila in the foyer.

Wiping her hand in her apron, she said, "Guest room is back this way."

The entire house had the shiny white tile floor, protected by big, colorful area rugs. Furniture was natural wood, not stained, a little rough, weathered. Paintings of buffalo hung on every wall. Two of the clocks were wagon wheels.

The home somehow managed to pay homage to the Old West past, even as it had a modern appeal.

"Your house is lovely," he said, following Sheila down a long hall.

"Oh, thank you. Decorating this was how Cole and I learned to compromise." She laughed. "Remodeling it, we learned how to compromise even more."

He laughed. "Marietta and I did some compromising around her purchase of a condo."

She paused. "Really? She let you help choose her condo?"

"Sort of. I went to see a few with her and gave her my thoughts. She made the actual decision."

She studied him. "That's still more opinion than she lets other people have." She laughed. "She's headstrong."

She opened the door on a big, airy bedroom. Sliding glass doors showcased a patio area. Off to the right, he could see a pool with a tall sliding board.

The doors were so big and everything was so close, he felt like he'd be sleeping outdoors.

But he said nothing. When Sheila guided him to the patio where everyone had congregated, he'd been given a beer and shown the refrigerator in the outdoor kitchen so he could help himself— like family, Sheila had said.

Like family.

He understood that because of how the Salvaggios had welcomed them into their life, but this felt different. First, there were about four times as many people. Second, there were kids and adults. Neighbors.

Danny and Junior joined him. "So. I hear you own a Bentley."

He shrugged. "Yeah. It's my favorite car."

"You probably have a sports car, too."

"Lamborghini."

"Oh, sweet."

The conversation shifted from cars to investments, and he realized that the big ranch that didn't seem to have any cattle did very well for itself.

"The clincher," Junior said, "was putting in the meat-packing plant."

Danny pointed behind them. "It's the biggest outbuilding off on the horizon. Now we control every step of the process. It's also a way to eliminate a middleman and cut costs."

Rico said, "I hear that," glad that they'd made a connection. Her brothers might dress more casually, but the business principles they operated on were the same Rico way guided his own investments.

He took a slow, happy breath. Just as Marietta had predicted, he did get along with her brothers.

But looking around, taking in the ranch and the people, watching Juliette and Sheila laughing as if they were longtime friends, knowing they had to have met because of Marietta, he realized something odd.

These people could have afforded to buy Marietta a condo. Yet she'd lived in an apartment with three roommates.

They adored her. One of her brothers almost always had his arm slung across her shoulders. Too many times to count, he'd seen her mom glance at Marietta with love in her eyes.

Yet she'd left them and lived virtually hand-to-mouth for five long years.

Her mother had said she was headstrong, but combining everything he was learning here to his own dealings with her, he had a sense she was a little more than headstrong.

The sun grew hotter, as Cole had predicted it would, and the kids put on swimsuits and filled the air with screams of delight as they splashed in the pool.

When her brothers left him, Marietta came over and sat by him. "Sorry, I sort of stranded you."

"I've been having interesting conversations with your family."

She winced. "Ouch. I can only imagine what they said."

"Nothing bad." He caught her gaze. "In fact, you seem like the favorite child."

"Oh, I am," she admitted without hesitation. "I'm the only girl."

He snorted.

"Hey, where we come from, dads and daughters, brothers and sisters?" She shrugged. "It works in my favor."

He glanced at her father again. He stood by an odd patch of land that not only had smoke meandering out in puffs, but also was covered in big leaves. He was the only one of Marietta's immediate family that Rico hadn't had a conversation with.

"Hey, Marietta," Juliette called. "Get over here and solve an argument—"

She glanced at him. He shook his head with a laugh. "Go. This is your family time."

He rose from the chaise lounge at the same time she did. "I think I'll get another beer."

Strategically, he got two and walked over to her dad and the patch of land that seemed to be on fire but no one cared.

He handed the beer to her dad, who said, "Thank you."

"You're welcome." He glanced around. The weird feelings about Marietta living in a cheap apartment haunted him. He understood that she was stubborn, but he couldn't see this big, brawny Texan letting his little girl live below their means. Given that he couldn't come right out and ask, he decided to edge his way to that with simple conversation.

He pointed at what looked to be dry leaves. "This is interesting."

Cole gave him a confused frown. "There's a pig in the ground, son."

Okay. That was odd. "A pig in the ground?"

"You've never had a piece of pork that was roasted this way?"

He just looked at him.

"Seasoned with garlic and simmering in the ground for twelve hours... Mmm. You are in for a treat."

Dear Lord, he hoped so.

A few seconds went by, then Cole said, "You seem to really like my little girl."

Seeing his opening, Rico sat on an available lawn chair and Cole sat on the one beside it. "I do. She's smart and funny." He didn't mention her cute accent since everyone in the family seemed to have one. "And strong. One of the strongest people I know."

Cole sniffed. "Yeah. She's smart and strong all right."

"You don't think so?"

"Took her a while to leave that jackass she was married to."

Rico held back his surprise. He absolutely wouldn't mention that Marietta had told him the jackass had left her. She might have let it appear that way to save face.

"But I will give you that she's strong. Took a lot

of guts to move away. Wouldn't take a dime of our money. Insisted she would make it on her own."

"And she did."

And her dad let her.

He still couldn't quite come to terms with that.

Cole gave him the side-eye. "I heard you paid for half the condo."

Feeling oddly like that was a condemnation, Rico said, "It's my child too and I wouldn't let her get a condo where she had to walk up four flights of stairs."

Cole laughed. "I'll bet that was an argument."

"Not really. I sort of gave her enough time to think it through and she realized I would be paying child support anyway and that meant she could afford something nicer."

There was respect in Cole's voice when he said, "It *is* a nice condo."

Rico held back a wince wondering if this guy had also seen him sleeping on the floor in front of the fireplace. Deciding it was best not to ask, he said, "Yeah. She did a good job picking it out."

"You give her space?"

Realization struck him. Rico had easily seen the end result of her bad marriage was an unbridled need to be independent. But he would bet her family had needed a little more time to figure it out. And that they'd made some mistakes in the process. "You don't?"

"Oh, we do now. At first, we weren't so smart

about how we dealt with her. Her ex was a piece of work. She never saw it. When she did, it was too late. He'd all but ruined her. She was shy. Hesitant. Afraid of her own shadow." He huffed out a breath. "She'd needed to go away. Sheila calls it finding herself. Made me promise not to interfere." Cole peered over at him. "You seem to be good for her."

"I think her job, Juliette's trust and Riley's friendship probably were better for her than I've been."

"Interesting. So you're saying you found her at just the right time."

He laughed. "Maybe."

Cole patted his knee. "Nope. I think you did. It all feels right to me." He pulled in a breath and hoisted himself out of his chair. "Pig's going to be done in about an hour. If you weren't dressed so fancy, I'd let you help get him out of the ground."

He wasn't sure what getting a hot pig out of the ground entailed, but Cole had made it sound like a compliment or an honor to be part of things. "I have a T-shirt and jeans in my overnight bag."

"Well, go get 'em on, boy. I'm starving."

CHAPTER FOURTEEN

A WEEK LATER, Marietta was overseeing a proposal in a coffee shop near her condo. The proposer was a nervous investment banker who'd met his girlfriend in this very coffee shop when they both reached for the same chai tea latte.

Trevor Martin wrung his hands in distress. "I'm sorry she's late. I swear. Her friend *is* bringing her here."

"No worries," Marietta said, brushing her hands along his shoulders and straightening his tie. "It doesn't hurt for you and me to have an extra minute to run through what's going to happen."

"You have the guy dressed up as a big cup of chai tea latte?"

"Absolutely." And he'd paid dearly for it, but apparently there was a running joke between him and Eloise about the talking latte. Marietta didn't have to understand people's inside jokes. She only had to fulfill their wish for a perfect proposal.

He glanced outside through the big glass storefront. "Here she comes."

186 ONE-NIGHT BABY WITH THE BEST MAN

Marietta said, "Places, everyone!"

The prospective groom raced to the counter and ordered two chai tea lattes.

The barista giggled. Everybody behind the counter tittered in anticipation.

Marietta slid into the background. The soon-to-be bride's parents waved at her, and she waved back. Friends and family of the happy couple filled most of the tables. It had also cost the groom a pretty penny to clear out the coffee shop for the fifteen-minute proposal so that all the tables were filled with friends and relatives.

The door opened. The two women entering chatted happily. The unsuspecting future bride innocently bopped inside. The friend who had lured her to the coffee shop winked at Marietta, who had blended into the crowd in the back of the room.

The bride walked up to the counter. "Chai tea…" She looked around. "Hey, this is the coffee shop where I met Trevor."

The man dressed in a huge coffee cup costume with "Chai Tea" written across the front said, "Did someone say chai tea?"

Everyone in the crowd laughed.

The bride-to-be finally saw her prospective fiancé. "Trevor?"

"That's my chai tea," Trevor joked.

Everyone laughed again.

The bride suddenly noticed that everyone in the room was someone she knew.

Trevor got down on one knee, opening a ring box. "I promise to always let you have the chai tea if you'll marry me."

She pressed her fingers to her lips. Her friend stepped back to get out of the pictures Layla was taking and the video Jake was filming.

"Yes! Yes! I'll marry you!"

The big cup of chai tea began to dance. Friends and relatives got up from the tables and approached to congratulate the happy couple.

Marietta stayed in the back, but she smiled. Another good proposal in the books. She watched them hug their parents and siblings, so happy, each had tears in their eyes. They were both in their midthirties but Marietta saw only their innocence. They naively believed that this happiness would last forever. But wait until the first time she burned his toast.

For some reason or another the bride's mother suddenly morphed into her mom. The bride's dad into her dad. She remembered her proposal with stunning clarity—

Her stomach soured. Her ex might have planned the most wonderful proposal, outside, spring birds chirping, family and friends laughing and weeping with joy, but the marriage had been a disaster.

Painful.

Filled with anxiety and depression.

Marietta gulped in a quick breath. She'd done at least a hundred proposals in the past year and not once had she had this kind of reaction. Remembering her own proposal? Superimposing her own family over the bride's? What was that—

The answer hit her quickly. *That* was the result of seeing Rico with her family. Once he and her brothers had clicked, there was no stopping him. He swam with the kids, helped get the pig out of the pit and absolutely charmed her mother by making blueberry pancakes for breakfast Sunday morning.

He fit with her family as if he belonged there.

Her chest tightened. All the air seemed to disappear from the room.

Not just because she didn't want to get married again, but because Rico fitting in lent a certain permanence to their situation.

Or made her the bad guy if she didn't want him coming to Texas with her or if she tried to put some distance between them.

"Marietta?"

At the sound of Jake's voice, she shook her head and brought herself out of her confusing thoughts. Rico had his own life. He had no intention of taking over hers.

"What's up?"

"We're done and the coffee shop owner says we have five minutes before our time is all used up. He wants his space back."

"You have the video and Layla has the pictures. The happy couple is laughing. I'd say our work here is done." She handed her clipboard to Layla. "Just let me say our goodbyes to everyone."

She walked toward the newly engaged couple but stopped suddenly, facing Layla and Jake again. "You two can go back to the office if you're ready."

Jake said, "Okay," and headed for the door. Layla followed him. In seconds they disappeared up the busy Manhattan street.

Marietta approached the future bride and groom, shaking her head. It was weird that she'd zoned out like that. Not just imagining her family but also forgetting to dismiss Layla and Jake. It wasn't like her to get distracted. People who wanted to keep their jobs stayed focused. And she could not afford to lose her job, her independence.

It would never happen again.

When Rico called her that night, as he did most nights, she even more clearly understood why all those strange things had happened to her that day. She and Rico were getting too close. Close enough that their situation reminded her of her first marriage, and close enough that worry about Rico edging his way into her life had sounded through her brain like a warning.

Maybe it was time to put some real distance between them?

When he called the following night, she didn't

pick up. He left a message, and she didn't return his call until late that night when she knew he'd be fast asleep in London. She told him she was extremely busy and suggested that he not come to Manhattan that weekend.

"I'll be doing two proposals a day. It's springtime. Everything's starting to bloom so people see the nice scenery as the perfect chance to have a beautiful setting for their proposal."

She disconnected the call feeling odd. Not like a liar...because she did have many proposals to oversee that weekend. The odd feeling was more like confusion. Telling him not to visit was the right thing to do—

So why did she feel horrible?

Rico had no problem with not going to Manhattan that weekend. He almost wondered how they'd gotten into the habit of spending so much time together—except he had a plane and a very uncomplicated life. He could pretty much be anywhere he wanted to be anytime he wanted to be there. He'd simply taken advantage of his freedom.

But after replying to his phone messages with texts all week, she begged off the next weekend and the one after that. Though he hated that they were talking through technology, not to each other, Rico refused to let himself be suspicious. She had a job. It was spring, April now. Her weekends were full of proposals and her weeks were filled with planning those events.

Respecting her workload, he didn't call her at all that week and, taking a page from her book, Friday afternoon he didn't call but texted about coming to Manhattan that weekend. Seconds later, he sighed as he read her text that she was too busy again for him to visit, but as he tossed his phone to a nearby table, it rang.

Hoping it was Marietta saying she'd changed her mind, he scooped it up, then frowned when he saw it was Antonio.

"Hey, Antonio. What's up?"

"GiGi's throwing a party tomorrow afternoon. It's last-minute, outside in the big entertainment area. It's not warm enough to swim but it will be fun to get together with all our friends. You can come, right?"

He thought of his disappointing text from Marietta and sighed with relief that he had something to get his mind off that.

"Yes. I'm totally free." So free he was excited over an unexpected invitation? To stay at the home of his friend's *grandmother*? That was so wrong he almost couldn't believe what he was feeling.

Or maybe he couldn't believe what he'd been doing. He'd thrown himself so far into Marietta's life that it had taken him weeks to realize she didn't want him there.

Glad he'd caught himself before he did something really off the wall, he called his pilot, packed a bag and was in GiGi's social room a few hours later, holding a glass of wine. Antonio was already there with Lorenzo and Juliette. The party was scheduled for the next day in the outside entertainment space, but it was good to be with his friends and feel normal again. Not like an unwanted guest—

Though Marietta had never made him feel unwanted and she'd been thrilled the weekend they'd visited her parents. Her family had loved him.

None of it made any sense.

Riley suddenly burst into the room, as if she'd run to get there.

She sat in the big chair with Antonio, and he kissed her cheek. "Okay, now?"

"Sure." She smiled weakly. "I'm fabulous."

GiGi said, "Rico, this is why we're glad you could come a day before the party."

Lorenzo and Juliette sat up weirdly, as if coming to attention. Antonio grinned. Riley said, "We're going to have a baby too!"

Rico blinked. "What? That's amazing! Marietta will be so thrilled!"

He rose to shake Antonio's hand as Riley said, "Oh, she was thrilled. She's talking about video calling and making tons of visits so our kids will know each other."

Though it gave him a weird jolt to realize Marietta had known about this baby before he did—known and hadn't told him—he hugged Riley.

But after a quick embrace, she pulled away and fell to her chair again as if dizzy. "I may have to miss dinner."

Juliette raced over to check on her.

Antonio said, "She has terrible *morning* sickness…that lasts all *day*."

"Marietta hasn't really been sick at all." Rico felt like a fraud saying that. How did he know Marietta hadn't been sick? He hadn't seen her in weeks. Sure, January and February seemed to go okay. But he'd barely seen her in March. What if she'd been keeping him away because she didn't feel well?

"Yeah, she's amazing," Juliette said. "You wouldn't even know she was pregnant. She's like a busy bee. She wanted to be here but apparently getting engaged in April has become a thing in Manhattan."

A weird sensation passed through Rico. He hated hearing about the mother of his child secondhand, from her boss.

But that was their life, the way they'd decided to live—

No. It wasn't. They'd decided to continue their romance until it ran its course. They'd promised to be honest when their feelings dimmed or died.

But if her feelings had dimmed or died, she hadn't said that. She'd used work as an excuse to get him out of her life and—damn it—he was not accepting that. If she wanted out, she had to say it. That was their promise to each other.

The reverse marriage vows.

Still, he couldn't leave the Salvaggios when they were having a party for Antonio and Riley to announce their good news. But Sunday morning? He was out of here.

Marietta had some explaining to do.

CHAPTER FIFTEEN

HE LEFT FLORENCE so early that with the time difference he arrived in New York just after sunrise. It took an hour to get from the airport to Manhattan. Coffee shops and newspaper stands were open and doing business on the warm Sunday morning, giving him an idea. If Marietta wasn't awake when he arrived, he could make breakfast. The scent of bacon would wake her slowly and she'd be fully conscious by the time she came out into the kitchen. He would not surprise her.

Just to be sure, he sent her a text before he opened her apartment door with the key she'd given him the day she'd moved in. He'd been taken aback by the gesture, but she'd said that as their baby's dad, he should have access to the house, just in case.

He wasn't sure what "just in case" entailed, but he knew what she meant. Still, that made her refusal to see him the past few weeks even odder.

He carried the bacon, eggs and bagels that he'd

bought in an open convenience store to the center island, not hearing a sound from her bedroom.

Shrugging out of his jacket, he headed for the stove and found appropriate frying pans, but before he even lit a burner, she came up the hall yawning.

"What are you doing here?"

Her voice sounded so wonderful that he couldn't turn from the cabinets. He needed a minute to get control of the emotions that burned through him. Need for her collided with the knowledge that she hadn't wanted him here. And he knew today would be the day he would confront her about forcing him to stay away. They would make decisions. Most of them not in his favor. And God only knew when he'd see her again.

His heart stuttered as he said, "I'm about to make breakfast. I sent you a text."

"I saw it. But aren't you supposed to be in Florence?"

His pain increased with the reminder that she knew things about him because of the Salvaggios and the Salvaggios knew things about *her*, about his baby, because of Riley.

The horrible feeling of being left out, being that foster kid who didn't belong anywhere, rumbled through him like a thunderstorm. He wasn't angry with Marietta or even the Salvaggios. It was more that he was tired of life treating him so shabbily… like an afterthought.

He turned to find her standing on the other side of the island, dressed in a T-shirt and yoga pants. Her hair billowed around her like a red-blond veil—then he saw it. Her stomach. The shirt, big as it was, had somewhere to fall, something to fit.

His heart stuttered. "You're showing?"

"Not really." She ran her hands down her belly, making the little bump obvious. "I have grown out of most of my pants, but I don't think I look pregnant."

He laughed. "Oh, you do. Just not to other people yet." He walked over and put his hands on her shoulders. "But I've seen that tummy flat as a pancake." His hands fell from her shoulders, down her arms and to the hem of her shirt. He slid them under the soft material to the swell of their child.

"Oh, my God. It's…" He felt the softness of her skin that protected their child and the bump that was their child. "Amazing."

Emotion overwhelmed him and he pulled her to him, hugging her. "Are you sure you're okay? Riley's throwing up and looks like death warmed over."

"I'll tell her you said that."

Even though the rumor mill that passed between all the women who worked at Juliette and Riley's companies annoyed him, right now it made him laugh. "Seeing her made me worry about you."

He hugged her again, feeling things he could neither define nor describe. She looked fine, hail and healthy, but that was a blessing. Their baby was a blessing. Marietta was a blessing, and he couldn't stop hugging her.

If they were breaking up today, he wanted one last chance to be with her.

A hug had never felt so good to Marietta. She hadn't seen him in a month. Hadn't let herself actually speak to him. Only listened to the sound of his voice in his increasingly short messages. And she knew he had grown weary of her avoiding him.

To have him here, holding her, made her want to weep. She melted into him, unable to stop herself, as tears filled her eyes and the sense of rightness billowed around them.

But she told herself it was pregnancy hormones, even though she allowed herself to stay right where she was enveloped in his arms, happy for the first time in weeks.

The joy of seeing him collided with the cold, hard fear of losing her independence, being subject to someone else's wishes and will, and formed a lump in her chest. As good as he felt, as desperate as she was to hold him, she knew the consequences of their staying close.

He very quietly said, "So, food first, or should

we go back to your bedroom and say hello properly?"

She wasn't as hungry as she was desperate. Half of her had longed to see him. The other half kept shouting warnings. Still, the warnings acted as a reminder that all of this was temporary. And she would know to be strong in the bad conversation that was to follow.

She stepped back, caught his hand and led him to her bedroom.

He stripped off his T-shirt the second they stepped into her room. His jeans followed. But when she reached to remove her T-shirt, he caught her hands.

"Let me." He laughed. "It's like unwrapping a present."

Guilt filled her. He liked this. Liked her. But she would have to put an end to it before she got in too deep...or he did. That was her real fear. She always knew to hold back, but he sometimes tumbled over into emotions because he didn't have a bad marriage in his past to show him how dangerous they were. With little to no knowledge of family, he was the wild card.

He lifted her shirt over her head, tossing it away before he bent and kissed her breasts. His lips then followed a path to her stomach. They smoothed over her baby bump reverently. Then he looked up at her and smiled. "This is amazing."

She agreed. It was amazing. And she was going

to shatter when he had to leave her as a companion and only connect with her as their baby's dad. But it was the right thing to do, better than losing her independence.

He eased away from their baby bump and rose to kiss her. Wrapping her arms around his shoulders, she allowed herself the pleasure of feeling him, memorizing the texture of his skin and the shape of his shoulders. He slid his hands to her bottom and rid her of the yoga pants before he eased her onto the bed with him.

He went slow. Tasting her. Teasing her. Sending electricity through her and regret. But she knew the right thing to do. Let him go. She took her turn enjoying the feel of him under her lips and fingertips and straddled him to complete their union. He took advantage of her position to cruise her skin, as if memorizing the shape of her. But that only increased her need until one final movement sent her over the edge.

They didn't drift apart. She couldn't. Knowing they were about to create those dividing lines for their relationship killed her. She rolled over to nestle against him as he laid his head on the pillow. His hand fell to her back and stroked softly.

"There is something we need to discuss."

She squeezed her eyes shut. For every bit that she knew this was necessary, it still hurt. "Yeah?"

"We made a promise to each other. I thought

that meant we wouldn't play games or hedge when it came to our relationship. I thought we were supposed to be honest when we no longer wanted to be romantically involved."

She took a long breath, not sure what he was saying. But before she could think of a reply, he added, "I don't understand. To me, it seems like our romance is alive and well. I mean, I know that attraction fizzles eventually, but I felt like we had a good year ahead of us before we tired of this."

He made a motion with his hand, sort of encircling them both, and her heart stuttered. She'd forgotten their deal. He hadn't. Even if he was having thoughts that went beyond raising the baby together, he didn't intend to act on them. He still wanted their deal. The one that assured they would walk away, wouldn't cling, wouldn't try to possess the other. The one that guarded her independence.

She said, "You give us a whole year?" Buying time as her brain continued to process the fact that he wasn't going to pressure her into something she didn't want.

"You don't? I mean, correct me if I'm wrong, but you seemed to have missed me."

She all but purred against him, as everything he said soaked into her emotion-filled brain and brought her to the conclusion that she'd misread him, misread what was happening between them. "I did."

"Then what was the cold shoulder about? You wouldn't even answer a phone call, let alone let me visit."

"I was busy." Not a lie. She was busy. And she felt foolish for jumping to the conclusion that Rico had changed his mind about their relationship. Then there was the matter that she hadn't fessed up to those fears or confronted him. She'd backed away—

A leftover from her awful marriage. Keith could never handle the truth. Avoidance became the way they communicated.

She suddenly realized how wrong that was. And that Rico was an honest guy who didn't want hard feelings between them. He wanted honesty.

Oh, God! The only way they could ever raise a child together would be if they were honest and she'd blown the first test!

She should have told him she worried he was getting too close.

"So is spring proposal season over?"

She laughed. A sense of lightness filled her. Rico would never trap her as Keith had. She could relax. Enjoy.

"I'm afraid spring proposal season is in full swing and when it ends summer proposal season will start."

He snorted. "That's some job you have."

She nestled against him and traced a circle on his chest. "Actually, it's a fabulous job. Layla may be leaving us when she graduates NYU. But we're training Jake to handle proposals on his own."

"The videographer with the long hair who's always in jeans?"

"Yes. We can hire another person to video the proposals. But he's seen so many in the past two years that he could oversee the simpler ones. As he gets better, he could plan and oversee more complex ones."

Still skeptical, he said, "The guy in the jeans?"

She laughed and playfully punched him. "Yes. You don't have to be romantic and bubbly to fulfill someone else's wishes. You have to listen. He does. You have to do what they want. He follows directions wonderfully. And you have to show up. No one is better at showing up than Jake is."

"Okay. Jake it is… Does this mean you're going to have free time?"

She nodded. "By summer…yes."

"That's great!"

"I'm going to have this child in late September. I'll need a few months off, time to establish a routine and hire someone to watch the baby once I go back to work."

"I'll help."

Unafraid now that she knew he didn't want anything permanent, only wanted to let their attraction run its course, she smiled at him. "You know, if you wanted to…you could be here during the months I'm off."

"I think I'd like to be here a few weeks *before* you have the baby. You know…to make sure you get to the hospital. That kind of stuff."

She laughed and angled up to kiss him. "I'll know to get myself to the hospital."

"What if there's a complication?"

"Eh. Maybe it would be good to have you here."

He rolled his eyes. "Other women would be thrilled if the father of their child took this much interest."

Seeing the disappointment on his face, she sobered. She shelved the sassiness that always helped her keep her distance and was honest with him, the way he wanted her to be.

"I am thrilled. I love that our child will have both parents. And I'll help establish a routine for you in London if you want."

"You'd be okay with me taking the baby to London?"

"Well, it might be better for you to visit here for the first year. But after that, our child should know how you live too. He should see your world, find his part in your life."

He nodded. "Makes sense."

She nestled against him again, totally relieved. They'd planned out an entire year. Technically, she'd made the dividing line. He wouldn't "live with" her for the full year after the baby was born, but she wouldn't stop him from having long visits if that was what he wanted. But after that year, everything would change. Their child would be able to visit him in London. There'd be no need for him to spend weeks or even weekends in Manhattan.

They now had an ending.

And she could relax and enjoy their relationship until that time came.

CHAPTER SIXTEEN

RICO HAD NEVER been happier. With the proposal planning business being what it was, he decided to go to London on the weekends and spend weekdays at her house. He got into the habit of picking her up after work, and because he had a car, he found himself carting her and Jake to venues for nighttime proposals.

But he didn't mind. He enjoyed feeling like part of her life. He got to know Juliette better. He watched Jake go from being a kid in blue jeans who took the videos to being the guy in dress slacks and a white shirt *overseeing* the kid who took the videos.

Watching him in the back corner of a restaurant where a doctor had just proposed to his girlfriend and a string quartet was entertaining the crowd of well-wishers and other restaurant patrons who'd loved seeing the proposal, Rico faced Marietta. "You have a good eye."

"Because I knew to train Jake?" She shrugged. "I can't take credit. Riley suggested it even before she and Antonio got engaged. After that both of our worlds became a whirlwind, so it took us until now to implement that plan."

The string quartet stopped. Patrons went back to eating. The doctor and his new fiancée took their seats again.

Jake walked over to where Rico stood with Marietta.

Marietta hugged him. "That's it. That's the last proposal I'll supervise you. You did great. You're on your own now."

He said, "Thanks," and immediately loosened his tie.

"And you don't have to dress so formally for proposals. You can go back to wearing jeans, as long as you stay in the background."

"I always stay in the background. No one wants their proposal planner in their videos," Jake said.

"Which is why I mentioned you being able to dress down," Marietta said with a laugh. "Any way that you want to dress is fine. Actually, going back to your jeans might be a good idea. Guys relate to you. It's fun watching how you can so easily get them talking about what they want."

Jake snorted, then shook his head. "I've got to admit, it's a skill I never would have believed I have."

"Good."

Rico dangled his car keys. "Need a lift some-where?"

"No. I'm going back to the office. You and Marietta can head home. I'll walk."

He said goodbye and left the restaurant. The happy couple who'd gotten engaged also left, snuggled together, happy, settled.

Watching them, an unexpected longing for that kind of contentment rippled through Rico. He was sort of dating, sort of living with, definitely having a baby with a woman who was very happy when he was around. She'd whisper the naughtiest suggestions to him when they talked on the phone the weekends when he was in London. She was openly affectionate.

But she was happy with things the way they were. She didn't want anything permanent. Even suggesting they should make some kind of commitment would probably send their relationship into a tailspin.

And what did it matter? He was happy too. He didn't need to muddy the waters by wanting something permanent. He was a grown-up with a very good life. The life he wanted—

That thought brought him up short again. Not because he hadn't thought that before, but because right now, in this moment, the simple idea that he had the life he wanted seemed to take on a deeper, richer meaning.

This really was the life he wanted.

Staying in Manhattan on weekdays, instead of weekends, he met Ethan O'Banyon for lunch every Wednesday. He'd bought an SUV to keep in the hangar he'd rented for his plane. He slept with Marietta, made her breakfast, took her to work—

Good Lord. He was putting down roots. He was doing happy couple things. His subconscious was pointing that out because changing their life without even realizing it was how people got hurt—

Except he couldn't see it ending in hurt. He couldn't see them ending at all. They fit. He fit into her life. She hadn't had to change a thing to add him into her world. And he'd found his place there. They *were* living as a happy couple.

As Marietta collected her things to leave the restaurant, the realization coalesced. He didn't have the sense that he should protect himself. After years of guarding his heart, keeping his distance, he'd found the place he wanted to stay.

Forever.

But he didn't dare tell her that.

The following night, they were proposal free, so they left the office a little after six and got into his SUV.

"Dinner?"

She shrugged. "It's early. Besides, I'm tired. Maybe we order a pizza?"

He glanced down at her increasing belly. She was heading toward six months along now. Only about ten pounds heavier. But he noticed that she tired easily. And he also noticed that he liked taking care of her, as they casually lived their lives like two people who belonged together. Even though neither one of them acknowledged that.

He started the SUV. "Pizza it is."

She relaxed against the seat with a sigh. "Good." She took a breath, then faced him. "My mom's birthday is next week so Dad's having a party on Saturday."

"Oh…"

So much for having the perfect life. With their living arrangements the way they were, he didn't know if she was telling him she'd be in Texas or asking him to go with her.

"I realize you like spending weekends in London because of my work schedule, but I know she'd love it if you'd come."

She'd love it if he'd come. Her mom. They weren't just a couple. Marietta made him sound like family.

But he didn't think Marietta realized how casually she'd included him. Which totally baffled him. Unless she was growing out of her fear of a commitment? They were happy. Their life was easy. Maybe she was changing her beliefs the same way he was changing his?

Still, this wasn't the time to ask. He wasn't even sure of his feelings yet. And the last thing he wanted to do was push her to the point that she kicked him out of her life again.

"Is your dad roasting a pig?"

"Now, don't get spoiled. He doesn't do a pig for every party." She laughed. "But he is for this one."

"Sweet."

She laughed again and took out her phone to order a pizza. By the time they got to her building, it had been delivered. They gave a slice to Tony, that night's doorman, along with a tip for accepting the order for them.

They ate the pizza in front of the TV and when they crawled into bed she fell asleep almost immediately.

He lay beside her watching the slight rise and fall of the covers as she breathed. A sense of comfort stole through him. Peace like he'd never known. And the final piece of the puzzle tiptoed through his brain.

He belonged.

Not just with her family. Not just in her life as a helpmate. But with her.

With her.

The absolute surety of it stole his breath. He'd never had a thought like that. Never. He'd always been so sure there was nowhere that he belonged. No one he belonged to or belonged with.

But he belonged with her.

He loved her.

Holy hell. He loved someone. He'd never felt this way about anyone or anything…but his instincts told him this was love.

* * *

They flew to Texas that weekend and arrived at the ranch house like family, not visitors. He knew the way to the room where he took their luggage. Her mom kissed him hello. Her dad slapped his back and told him to come outside and sit by the pig with him.

He soaked in the sense of belonging. He knew it was an extension of his feelings for Marietta. But he also knew that while his feelings with her family were dependent on his feelings for her, his feelings for her weren't dependent on outside forces.

He loved her. And if keeping her in his life meant never mentioning that, that was a sacrifice he'd make.

It killed him to recognize that it was the right thing to do. He'd never felt this kind of love or the urge to tell her, to act on it, but the last thing she wanted was a commitment.

He and her father stepped outside to a blue sky that allowed an unrelenting sun to bathe them in warmth. Guests began arriving with Jell-O salads, three-bean salads, cookies and cupcakes—and gifts. What looked like hundreds of gifts piled on a table to the right of the buffet that also grew with every guest. The air shimmered with heat and friendship.

Rico sat back in his Adirondack chair.

"So, baby in a couple of months?"

The question came from her brother Junior, who had come over to join Rico and Cole. Even before he answered, Danny walked over too.

Accustomed to her family's way of talking, shortening sentences, eliminating verbs sometimes, he said, "Yes. In a few weeks, we'll start putting together a nursery." Talking about the baby, he could see his and Marietta's life together stretching before them in a never-ending wave. He wasn't going to quibble over the word *commitment*. Sometimes actions were better than ceremonies.

"You gonna move from London?"

That question was a little trickier. He'd probably never sell his house in London, but he'd be living with Marietta. It would happen naturally and continue forever. He had absolutely no doubt of that.

His gaze found her in the crowd, laughing with her mom and sisters-in-law. She looked at him and smiled.

Yeah. They would be together forever. Just without the rings.

"I'll be keeping the house in London. But I also intend to help Marietta raise the baby. I'll be in Manhattan a lot."

As if she could read his mind, her pretty smile grew.

Dear God. He really loved her. The feeling was so amazing it nearly overwhelmed him.

Breaking the spell, he shifted his gaze to her dad. "I can work from Manhattan, but, you know, I've been in London for over fifteen years. I don't want to get rid of that house. A person can have more than one house."

Cole batted his hand. "Billionaires. You guys kill me. You've gotta have a house everywhere. Tell me something. Do all your houses feel like home?"

Rico chuckled, but the question fit with all the thoughts he'd been having. He'd never actually had a home. He'd had foster homes that gave way to living under a bridge that gave way to living in crappy apartments that gave way to better apartments that eventually became the London house—

But none of them had ever felt like home. They were symbols of where he was financially. Stepping stones.

Living with Marietta felt like home.

Living with Marietta *was* home.

The conversation slowed and her two brothers drifted away to get their kids out of the pool or greet new guests.

Cole pulled in a long, content breath. And why not? His house was filled with happy friends and neighbors. His wife loved him. His sons worked the family business. They all adored Marietta. They were a family.

"Are you ever going to make an honest woman out of my daughter?"

Rico almost choked on his beer at the abruptness of the question. He would like nothing better than to marry Cole's daughter, but he knew life didn't always give a person everything they wanted. He would be content with what they had.

"She wouldn't be happy to hear you ask me that. Besides, that's an outdated attitude."

"Yeah. Yeah. I know. You and Marietta are very hip."

Rico snorted at Cole's use of the word *hip*.

"Come on. Sell that house. Move to Manhattan. I know you want to."

He did.

But he also respected Marietta's wishes. Meaning, he also wouldn't discuss them with her dad.

"My house in London is home base."

Cole's face scrunched in confusion. "What does that even mean?"

"It's…you know…if someone wants to find me that's where they look."

"Or they could call your cell phone. You don't have to have a home base anymore. People can reach you from anywhere anytime," Cole said with a laugh, but he sobered suddenly. "All joking aside, Rico, I've never seen Marietta this happy. It's as if her past didn't happen. I don't know you well, but I can see you're happy too. Not sure what kind of sign you two think you have to get to tell you that you need to make a commitment, but you do. You and my daughter created a child, and kids need security. They need to know you are going to be around to keep them safe and make their supper." He rose from the seat. "I know I sound like a meddling old man right now…but in Texas a dad's got the right to say his piece. That's mine. My daughter loves you. Intentional or not, you started a family. Make it official."

Cole left and Rico found Marietta in the crowd and joined her conversation, but Cole's words haunted him the rest of the afternoon. Not because he didn't like Marietta's dad's interference, but because deep down Rico knew he was right. He loved Marietta and when she snuggled against him in bed that night with a contented sigh, he knew she loved him too.

He didn't want to push her into something she didn't want. But was it really out of line to help her to see they belonged together?

It might not be. He looked at their relationship as evolving and if her dad was to be believed, being together had changed her too.

Still, he didn't know that for sure.

Driving to the airport the next day, Rico sneaked a peek at her. He felt things for her he had never believed existed, but they also had a deal. Still, that might actually be the way to approach this. From the vantage point of their deal.

He suddenly had a flash of guilt for wanting a

commitment with someone who'd made it clear she didn't want one.

Worse, he had no idea what he would do if she said no.

The last time she'd thought they were getting too close she'd kept them apart for almost a month.

That was the risk he was facing.

But the other risk was that they'd fall apart or drift apart. There were too many ways they could drift apart if they didn't at least have a commitment conversation, and he didn't want that. He wanted to grow old with her.

He really and truly wanted to ask her to marry him.

The conclusion surprised him so much he could have wrecked the car, but it was right. He knew it was right.

CHAPTER SEVENTEEN

THE FOLLOWING WEEKEND, with Rico in London, Marietta's condo echoed with silence. She reminded herself that a baby would fill her house with noise and happiness, but her thoughts took a horrible turn.

She began imagining herself as an abject failure as a mom. Most of her thoughts were based on the horrible insults her husband would hurl at her when she couldn't get pregnant.

You can't do anything right.
You're worthless.
You're weak.

She wasn't weak. She was strong.

She was strong enough that she hadn't had thoughts like these in years. Literally years. They could have been from normal fear as her due date approached or maybe pregnancy hormones, but realistically she knew making two trips to Texas so close together had probably brought them back. Memories of dating Keith and getting married in her parents' backyard had risen from her subconscious, but being pregnant seemed to make them worse.

Like it or not there was a connection between a baby and her ex. The baby she couldn't give to him. His anger and outbursts. That was when the insults would fly. Normally, a person would think that being pregnant should end all her doubts. After all, her getting pregnant pointed to the idea that perhaps Keith was the one who couldn't conceive. Instead, being pregnant seemed to bring back her insecurities.

And that was wrong.

That was also why people had friends. Riley would remind her that she was fine. Better than fine. She was pregnant. She had a new job where she was a leader. She had a home. A condo she'd purchased.

She walked back to the soon-to-be nursery, which currently housed a table for her laptop and a comfortable chair. She ambled to the comfortable chair and hit a few keys on the laptop to video call Riley.

She answered on the first ring. "Hey!"

"Hey! I didn't expect you to answer so quickly."

"I was working on my computer… I'm thinking about adding a new arm to the business."

"Are you up to that? I know you've been sick."

Riley studied her friend. "I was. That's mostly gone now, but we'll talk about that in a minute. Your eyes are tired. Are you not sleeping?"

"I'm fine. I'm just…having some thoughts."

"Thoughts?"

"Yeah. Remembering things my ex-husband would say when we couldn't get pregnant." She batted a hand. "You know what? It's foolish stuff. Things that I know aren't true. I'm fine."

"You aren't fine, or you wouldn't have called me. Just talk about it. You'll feel better."

She sucked in a breath. "Okay. Honestly, I know being pregnant affects people differently. And I know going to Texas twice in the past few weeks has…you know, brought some things to mind. But every time Rico goes to London, the quiet in the condo leaves an opening for thoughts to creep in."

"Makes sense," Riley answered casually. "That marriage was harder than you let on. You kept a lot inside and while another person might believe getting pregnant would prove once and for all your ex was wrong…reminders are a weird thing."

She blew her breath out on a sigh. "So, you agree that's it? That I'm just being reminded of things?"

"There are a lot of connections going on. Getting pregnant. Going to Texas. Thinking about being a mom. How could you not have a flashback or two from all those years you tried to get pregnant and couldn't?"

That was exactly what the thoughts were. Flashbacks. Not current or even applicable to what was happening now. Just old memories.

She laughed. "You're right."

"Tell the thoughts to take a hike," Riley said. "They're just thoughts. Just things a miserable man said to make you feel like you were to blame. We all know that you weren't."

She ran her hands down her face. "You're right. And seriously, the only time I think about these odd things is when Rico's in London."

Rico arrived at the Manhattan condo, using his key to let himself inside. He hadn't waited until Monday morning to leave London. He'd flown out early. He liked the daily ritual of taking Marietta to work. And, thanks to a long conversation with proposal planner Jake the week before, he also had a plan to ease changing their deal—committing to each other—into a discussion.

He'd actually met with Jake to arrange a proposal. He'd considered every possible way for him and Marietta to have the talk about making their relationship permanent and they all seemed blah. Worse, all of them gave her a way to push the discussion to another time. But watching one of Marietta's proposals, he'd realized that emotion always won the day at those events, and if he asked Marietta to marry him among friends and family, with him being sincere and vulnerable, their emotion would overwhelm them, and they'd hug and kiss and everything would be decided.

When he'd said it, Jake had winced.

"First of all, I think you two belong together. So getting married is a good thing."

Glad Jake agreed with him, Rico waited expectantly, until Jake said, "But you can't take her to Central Park and spring the idea of getting married on her. From what I hear, her first marriage was a mess, and she also likes to be in control."

Rico sniffed. "Yeah. I get that. But I'm out of ideas. We never even considered marriage when we got together. In fact, we sort of vowed we wouldn't do it. Now, I don't know how to bring it up. I thought maybe proposing in a really great way might get her to see we should get married."

Jake shook his head. "No. If she sprung a proposal on you that would work, but you proposing to her would be better if it happened naturally. And I think that's why you're out of ideas. I think life's trying to tell you to wait for the moment when the time is right. Be ready. Have the ring. Have the words. And wait for your moment."

Deep down, Rico knew all that. But he'd hoped Jake could come up with an adorable proposal that would somehow get around all the stuff they needed to handle. When he hadn't, Rico knew he was back to square one.

But, as Jake had said, he was ready. He was

now on the lookout for the right time, and he'd bought a ring in London.

The silence in her condo confused him until he walked down the hall, heading to the bedroom where he would leave his suitcase, and he heard Marietta talking.

Then he heard Riley's reply. "Maybe the thing to do would be not have Rico go back to London every weekend."

Rico stopped in the hall, just short of the open door. He didn't want to eavesdrop, but it sounded like the discussion was breaking in his favor.

"Oh, no. No. No. No. I was just thinking exactly the opposite. The only way I'll adjust to the quiet condo is if I experience it more."

He bobbed his head in silent agreement, seeing her logic. But her not liking the quiet of her condo could mean that she missed him a lot more than she let on.

Another point in his favor. Another way to start a conversation where they could reevaluate their relationship.

"Look, you can adjust to the quiet later. Right now, you have to get through this pregnancy. If having Rico around helps with that, I say solve today's problems today and handle tomorrow, tomorrow."

It wasn't just the quiet? She'd had a problem? When he was away? What kind of problem?

"It's just a bunch of wayward thoughts. Ideas

planted by a person who wanted to hurt me. Logically I know that. The best way to handle them is to learn to blot them out."

"Yeah, but I think there's more to your feelings when Rico's not around. I think you miss him."

"I do."

Riley laughed. "Because you like him."

"I do! I like him a lot."

Rico smiled. Things were definitely breaking in his favor.

"Honestly, Marietta, I think you two need to get married."

His heart about jumped out of his chest. He fingered the ring box in his jacket pocket. Everything Jake had said seemed to be taking shape. This really was beginning to feel like that spontaneous moment they needed.

Then he heard Marietta say, "We're fine as we are."

"You're not fine. You're in limbo. And you're not the kind of person to live in limbo. You make decisions. You take action. That's why you're feeling funny. You *want* the next step."

Rico stifled a sigh of relief. Things were back to looking good again.

He waited. If Marietta could work through all this on her own with Riley, the discussion of amending their deal and getting married would go a lot easier for him.

"I disagree about us getting married. And you

should too! We were just talking about what a creep Keith was. I don't want to get into that again."

Riley immediately came to his defense. "Rico's not like that."

"Not now."

His face scrunched in confusion.

"Just wait until things go wrong. Wait until he can't have his own way." She sucked in a breath. "I've seen the bad side of a great guy."

"Keith was not a great guy."

Antonio's voice calling for Riley came through the computer.

Riley said, "I'm in here."

"GiGi and I are waiting for you to come to dinner."

She winced. "Sorry. I must have been working longer than I thought."

Marietta shook her head. "No. I'm sorry. I didn't mean to keep you."

"Are you kidding? I love talking to you! And we can pick this up later if you want. We'll talk about something happier than your horrible ex."

Marietta laughed. "Okay. Maybe I'll call tomorrow."

Riley said, "Sounds good," then she disconnected the call.

Rico stood outside the bedroom door, his thoughts scrambled, his mind whirling. He didn't even have the brainpower to get himself away from the door. Just stood there as she walked out of the room.

Her eyes widened. "Rico!"

"I'm not that guy."

"What?" She studied him for a second and he watched recognition change her expression. "You heard our conversation."

"Only the last two minutes. I would have walked by the door, but Riley said something about you having a problem and I stopped. I wanted to hear it so I could help you."

She pulled in a breath. "I'm sorry if what you heard offended you."

"It didn't offend me. It confused me. I'm not your ex and I'm glad. I've heard nothing but crap about him every time I went to Texas. Your marriage didn't fall apart because you couldn't get pregnant. It fell apart because Keith was a narcissist."

"No. My parents like to think everything was Keith's fault, but there were issues. He started off a nice guy and our issues ruined him."

"Is that really what you believe?"

"Yes and no. I get it that he was self-centered and when things got complicated, he couldn't handle not getting what he wanted."

He released the ring box, let it fall from his hand and nestle into the soft material of his pocket.

This was not his moment. Not even close.

"But in the beginning, he was a good guy."

"You are more generous with him than I would have been. But what's interesting is that you gave him the benefit of the doubt. But you won't give me the benefit of the doubt. You're sure I'm going to become just like him."

"Maybe you're right." She took a breath. "But it doesn't matter. You and I have already been through this. We made a plan. We're going to have a baby and raise that child happily because we aren't going to let arguments and different needs get in the way. We're going to work together."

He watched her eyes for a few seconds because it was his turn to draw some conclusions. Their pact didn't just protect her from their relationship souring. She saw it as a wall. Something that completely separated them.

"And you think us getting too involved, or even liking each other too much, risks what we have?"

"It's not the 'liking' that's the risk. It's expectations that cause friction. We won't have that."

He stepped back, as the full force of what she said hit him. "No. If we're not supposed to like each other, or care enough about our relationship to try to straighten out points where we disagree, then we won't have any emotion at all."

"We'll have love for our child."

He nodded but his heart splintered into a million pieces. They couldn't go forward because she couldn't stop looking back, building barriers that prevented them from repeating what she saw as mistakes. He didn't question what she was saying or how she felt. Having been disappointed by love, he'd also shied away for years. But knowing her had changed him. Falling in love with her, thinking he finally understood love, those things had changed him.

But falling for him hadn't done that for her. Her disappointment with relationships didn't merely linger. It informed what she believed about love. It still colored how she looked at life. How she looked at *him*.

If the strength of what he felt didn't even make an impression, everything he believed he was experiencing was a mirage.

The sense of belonging.

Having a place.

Being in love.

Those had all been illusions.

He turned and headed toward the door again. This time was different—given that he had an expensive suitcase in hand, not a trash bag of his belongings as he'd always had when a foster home didn't work out—but the feeling of being let down was the same as he took the familiar long steps to get away.

It was the story of his life. Nothing was permanent. Especially not emotion. Or love.

She called after him. "You're going?"

"I think I'll stay uptown tonight and head home tomorrow."

"Wait!" Her voice was incredulous, not filled with fear or sadness. Only surprise that their discussion was causing him to leave. "You don't have to go."

He stopped, turned. "I think I do. At first, I thought we were on the same page about our relationship, so I couldn't believe you didn't see we were changing. But now I understand. We're looking at our situation two different ways. I sort of edged myself into your life, but you haven't even tried to fit me into yours." He sniffed a laugh. "I also see why. While I was finding things in common with you…making a connection, you were always holding back, keeping me in the place you thought I fit, keeping your world as close to what you wanted as you could." He turned back toward the door, but quickly pivoted to face her again. "I get it. I do. No one wants to wake up one day and find themselves in a bad relationship. I understand. You just don't feel for me what I feel for you."

He took a breath. "Call me if you need anything. But no more visits. In fact, when the baby's born, I'll get a nanny so I can have time with him or her on my own. We don't have to see each other again."

With that he left. He stepped through the door,

into the hall and stopped only long enough to take another breath to shift gears.

He wished he was angry. But he wasn't. He was familiar with rejection. He'd handled the hurt of it, the stinging pain of realizing he was on his own, hundreds of times before.

He would handle it again.

But this would be different. Maybe for the first time in his life, he had let himself love someone and she'd rejected him. Before, he could always say that as long as he held himself back the rejection wasn't personal, but this time he'd loved. He'd felt the joy of it. Now he felt the wave of pain.

And, again, even as it made him understand why she held back, it made the heartache immeasurably worse.

CHAPTER EIGHTEEN

MARIETTA WOKE ALONE—AGAIN. Only this time she knew it was permanent. She tried to tell herself that while being alone, being hurt, feeling empty was what she'd been trying to avoid, she couldn't escape the inevitable reality that she had landed here anyway.

Because that's what happened in relationships. People got hurt.

She rolled out of bed, showered and dressed, talking to the baby, who was active now. Twice she swore he or she had tried to punch her.

Sadness hit her. She didn't even know if her baby was a boy or a girl. They'd decided not to learn the sex of the baby because they'd wanted to be surprised together in the delivery room. But what fun would it be to be alone when she got the news?

Telling herself not to think about that, she took the subway to work and hurried to her desk. She told herself she wasn't hiding from the heartache of losing Rico and knowing she'd broken his heart. She simply had a lot of planning and budgeting and supervising to do. Luckily, the complexities of accounting would keep her so involved that nothing else would have a chance to sneak in.

The first week that Rico was gone, she'd convinced herself she was upset because she'd hurt him. The second week, when Marietta had fallen into full-fledged depression, she couldn't be so detached. She missed him. With lots of time to think through everything he'd said, she realized he could see their future as something more than them being polite to each other while they raised a child. He saw them sharing a house, bouncing their little boy or girl on their knee, fixing dinner, putting this child to bed, then sharing a bed.

She'd believed he was being dreamy or starry-eyed. But after another two weeks without him, she could see his vision and realize that it all sounded right.

Not because she hated being alone. That was just a symptom of a bigger issue. She loved him. Somehow love had sneaked by her defenses and she'd fallen. Almost accidentally.

When she'd come to that conclusion, it had knocked everything else out of her brain. They'd spent months together. It should not shock her that she'd developed strong feelings.

But as he'd said, she'd kept him at a distance. He'd eased his way into her world. She'd stayed out of his. As if she wanted no part of him. No wonder he'd been hurt.

She ran her hand across her forehead. He probably hated her.

If he didn't, he should.

She hadn't given an inch in their relationship.

That was supposed to protect her from this pain, but it hadn't.

Jake knocked on the frame of her office door. "I have last month's hours for you to approve."

She forced herself to look happy and chipper. "Need me to authorize overtime?" she teased.

His face reddened. "Actually, I'm not taking money. I'd like two mornings off to compensate for two of the nights I worked last week."

She took the spreadsheet he handed her. "Doctor's appointments?"

He winced. "Dates."

"Oh."

Embarrassed that she'd inadvertently delved into his personal life, she put her attention on his spreadsheet. Looking over the entries, she almost signed it. Then she saw *Mendoza=canceled*.

"Mendoza is Rico's last name."

His face reddened again. "I know."

Just the mention of his name sent longing through her. But Mendoza was a common name. She should have recognized that it could have been any one of the other hundreds of thousands of Mendozas in the greater New York area and let it alone. But something pushed her.

"Did he come to you for a proposal?"

"I don't feel right talking about it."

She arched one eyebrow. "I'm your boss. You're supposed to talk to me about every aspect of your job."

He winced. "Okay. He did want a proposal. But he canceled it."

Her heart sank. He was thinking about proposing to her?

"Actually, I should have taken it off my work page. The whole thing was a nonstarter. He came to me because he wanted a proposal, but I talked him out of it. The entire conversation wasn't more than fifteen minutes."

Common sense told her to end the discussion, as it was a moot point, but some Texas longhorn devil pushed her forward. "*You* talked him out of it?"

"Marietta, I told him he shouldn't spring a proposal on you. But I also told him you wouldn't want anything public. I told him a proposal to you should be intimate."

Her heart stuttered. She could picture it. "Oh."

He started to leave but turned back again. "My conversation with him ended with him agreeing and nothing came of it. I should have erased him from the sheet."

The thought of marrying Rico should have

scared her silly, but with four weeks to think about how much she missed him, and realizing he'd been hinting for more from their relationship, a personal, intimate marriage proposal sounded nothing but romantic.

She tried to bring herself back to reality with a reminder of her ex, but all she remembered was Rico telling her he wasn't that guy. He wasn't her ex. He wasn't like her ex.

Even thinking that he was, was insulting.

No wonder he'd stood his ground.

She'd insulted him.

A week later, she went home to a nursery that was filling with boxes of furniture that she would have to put together, or call her dad to put together.

But she couldn't think about her dad without thinking about how much he'd liked Rico. She leaned against the wall and slid down to the floor. How had she missed all this? How had she missed the signs of how perfect they were for each other?

Because she'd been falling for him, and she'd gotten scared. So she'd protected herself, refusing to see it.

He'd been moving forward, and she'd dug in her heels like a Southern belle on a rampage.

And she'd lost him because of it.

Weeks flew by like minutes for Rico. The only communication he'd had with Marietta was by text. She told him about doctor's appointments, setting up a nursery and hiring a nanny as neutrally as if she'd been telling him the weather.

It did not faze him. The final nail in the coffin of him believing in love had not only been pounded in; it was secure.

He'd always believed he was meant to be alone. The failure of his relationship with Marietta had proved it. He'd reached deep down into his memories and found the strength to go back to being the kid who understood that and made a good life anyway.

He scheduled six weeks off. The last two in September when the baby was due and four weeks in October to have time with his new child. But he wasn't staying with Marietta. He would get his usual hotel suite.

He arrived in Manhattan that sunny September day to find a car waiting for him. That was another thing he'd done. No more owning a vehicle when he was in the city, as if he belonged there. He didn't. He would have a driver at his disposal.

The chauffeur opened the door. He got in, got settled. With an hour's drive into the city, he opened his briefcase and began to work.

His phone rang.

He sighed, picking it up to dismiss the call. But he saw the caller was Juliette and he answered, "Hey, gorgeous! What's up?"

"Rico, I don't know where you are, but you

need to get here. Well, not the office, the hospital. Lorenzo and I are on our way out now."

He sat up. "Did something happen with Marietta?"

"Her water broke. Ambulance just took her to the hospital."

"Which hospital?"

She gave the name.

"I just landed at the airport. I'll be there in a few minutes."

"Lorenzo and I will see you there."

They disconnected the call. And for the first time since they'd decided to call it quits, he let himself think of Marietta. Her pretty smile, her wild hair, her stubbornness. He closed his eyes, remembering touching her, loving her.

He shouldn't have feelings for her. If anything, he should think of her like poison ivy and just want to stay away. But worry that something had gone wrong filled him. He had to get to her. He had to help her. He would let himself be neutral again after the baby was born and everything was fine. Because the baby would be okay and so would she. He wouldn't accept anything else.

But right now, she needed him and he would be there.

What felt like an eternity later, he got to the hospital and was directed to the maternity ward. After the typical hustle and bustle of racing through groups of people and riding an elevator, he experienced an unexpected quiet and calm when he arrived on her floor. He went to the desk and once again had to present ID.

Luckily, Lorenzo stepped out of one of the rooms and walked over to the nurses' station. "This is the father of Marietta Fontain's baby."

The nurse nodded. "Go ahead and show him down the hall, Lorenzo."

As they walked away from the nurses' station, Rico said, "Lorenzo? You're on a first-name basis with a nurse?"

He laughed. "It might be like Fort Knox to get in, but once you prove you belong here, the ward atmosphere is very friendly."

They walked into a room where Juliette stood beside Marietta's hospital bed. When she saw him, she stepped back, revealing the see-through bin in which a very tiny baby slept.

He just stared at Marietta and the baby.

Juliette eased Lorenzo out of the room. "We'll give you some privacy."

He walked closer to the bed.

Marietta's lips trembled when she said, "Don't be shy. We are fine and your son wants to meet you."

"I have a son?" Tears filled his eyes. He didn't know what to process first. The baby or the feeling of seeing Marietta again after weeks and weeks apart.

Knowing her feelings about him, though, he

held himself together, didn't give in to the emotions that swamped him. "You're okay?"

She made a strangled noise. "It seems I might lean toward spontaneous deliveries."

"Spontaneous deliveries?"

"My water broke. Juliette called an ambulance. I got to the hospital quickly and by the time they wheeled me up here, Henry was making his way into the world."

He stepped closer. "Henry?"

"Okay. Maybe not Henry. How about Neville?"

He inched closer and peered and across the bed at the red-faced baby. Everything suddenly felt real, not wooden, not the neat little package of strength he had wrapped himself in to protect himself. Wave upon wave of emotion flooded him.

"Oh, my God. That's our baby."

"Remember how you thought it was amazing that my stomach was growing?"

He remembered clearly. It was his first time of truly understanding that they were having a child, and probably the first time he realized that his feelings for her were inching beyond their deal.

He tried to fight those feelings now, but love for her hit him full force. He eased closer to the bed. "I remember."

"Well, holding the baby is a hundred times more amazing."

He didn't doubt that for a second. He had so

much trouble struggling against his longing for her that he knew once he held his child, he'd be overwhelmed.

He bought himself some time to pull himself together. "I don't like Neville either."

She laughed. "Yeah. You're right. It sounds very Broadway play to me. How about Stewart?"

His emotions began to click with reality. The baby. Being beside Marietta. Talking like normal people. Even though they were far from normal.

Standing so close to her, he couldn't deny that she was everything he'd always wanted. And maybe he should have fought for her.

But honestly, he hadn't known how. As broken as he was, she was worse. Raw and vulnerable. Leaving her had been the right thing.

Still, they both had to deal with the fact that he would be in her life while they raised their child. "I'm sorry I missed his birth."

She caught his hand and squeezed. The softness of her fingers wrapped around his nearly did him in. "You could have been right next door to the hospital, and you would have missed the birth. It wasn't worth the price of a ticket. He all but bounced on the diving board and jumped out."

He laughed, realizing how much he'd missed her Texas way of looking at life. All the reasons he'd fallen in love with her coalesced, reminding him of why he'd been so willing to take the risk on love when it had done nothing but treat him shabbily.

Still, that was the past. He had to deal with her differently now. Everything was about their child.

"I suppose I have a lot of things to apologize for."

She frowned at him. "Really? Like what?"

"Being so distant these past few weeks." It killed him that he'd stayed away. But standing here now, so close to her, he understood why he'd had to do it. He longed to love her, even more than he had before.

But she didn't want him, and he had to accept that. He had a child now to fill his life. He would make that enough and be grateful. "I was thinking maybe we should name him Cole."

She frowned. "After my dad?"

"I like your dad."

She smiled. "I like him too. And he'll be thrilled for a namesake. But what about Rico Cole."

"He sounds like a soft drink."

She laughed. "How about Cole Michael?"

"Cole Michael?"

"Like Michael the Archangel... If you don't like angels, Michael's simply a very nice name. Strong. But also cute." She frowned. "Oh, shoot. I can see my daddy calling him Mikie."

He tried out the name. "Mikie." He caught her gaze. "I like it."

* * *

Her eyes filled with tears. "I do too." He looked so good that her heart hurt. She'd also missed him so much that he could have been covered in dirt and wearing sackcloth and she'd have been happy to see him.

He headed toward the see-through bin in which little Mikie lay. He was finally going to meet his son. And it was her fault he hadn't been here for the birth. He'd wanted to spend the weeks before with her. Then she'd driven him away.

"Now I guess it's my turn to say I'm sorry."

Bent to pick up his son, he raised his head and glanced at her questioningly.

"That argument we had that ended us? That was all on me. You were right. I was afraid. I was judging you by my ex's behavior. I was wrong."

He looked away, not answering. Instead, he reached in, lifting the baby.

She understood why he wouldn't want to talk about that day and changed the subject.

"Rub your cheek against his," Marietta suggested. Though she tried to stop it, her heart swelled seeing him holding their son. "He's like velvet."

He brought their faces together and laughed. "Oh, my God, he's so soft."

This was it. Despite what had happened between them, he wanted to be part of their son's life and she had to do the right thing. "And he's gonna need a daddy hanging around."

"You might need dynamite to keep me away." He cuddled the baby again. "I almost can't believe it."

"Me neither," she said, her heart stuttering. Though she loved seeing Rico with the baby and knew he didn't want to talk about their argument, she couldn't just let things stand. She'd hurt him and he deserved to know how wrong she'd been. If she left out the argument, there was only one way to show him.

For all her bravado, she wasn't sure she had the chops for this. But she took a long breath and said, "I love you."

He peered over at her. "Do you want me to give you Mikie?"

She shook her head. "No. I wasn't talking to Mikie. I was talking to you." She paused only a second. "I do love you, you know."

He stared at her as if he didn't know what to say. Then the shattered look came to his eyes again and she was lost for a way to fix it. She'd made such a mess of things that she knew she had to be the one to make the first moves, say the right thing, rid them of the awkwardness.

She remembered the way he'd been thinking about proposing to her and knew just how much she'd probably broken his heart. In a world where very few people got a chance to make up for the wrongs they'd done, she actually had one. He might not have asked her to marry him, but she knew he'd wanted to.

And she really wanted him in her life again. Not as the father of her baby. As her everything. He'd seen it before she had, but now that she'd realized it, she also prayed they weren't permanently broken.

This was her chance, her moment. If this didn't set things right, nothing would.

She held his gaze. "I told you I love you because I want to marry you."

Rico stared at her. He'd stomped down his feelings for weeks, but the second he'd seen her, they had all come storming back. If she hurt him again, he wasn't sure he could survive it.

"Do you think this is the best time for you to be making a life decision? We're both a little overwhelmed right now."

She laughed. "Oh, honey. Sometimes the truth only stands out clearly when we're bombarded by other emotions."

He snorted. "You Texas people have a weird way of looking at life."

He cuddled his son. The click he'd felt the day he'd decided he wanted to marry her returned. The silly, happy emotion of it. He remembered her father's words about a child needing security, but it was the way she made him feel when he was with her that flooded him.

"I'm not saying yes."

Her eyes grew sad. "Okay."

"You're getting this all wrong. I do want to marry you, but I want to be the one to propose."

She peeked up at him. "Really?"

"Yes. And there are some things we need to talk about first. You know, we're going to fight sometimes, right?"

She laughed. "Probably not knockdown, drag-out fights, but yeah we'll disagree."

"And you still want to marry me?"

"Yes. But without the big to-do… I want what we have to be about us. Not how we look to other people. I want us to be honest and fair and talk about things. I want us to be together forever."

His heart melted. He knew what it had cost her to get to this point, but she'd gotten here, and he wouldn't make an issue of it. "That sounds good to me. I watched other people have families my entire life and fought the urge to want one myself. But you made me feel normal. Like I belonged. That's what I want."

"I think we just wrote our marriage vows."

He laughed. "Or maybe we just took the real vow that's going to keep us together. Though I wouldn't mind a small ceremony at the Salvaggios' vineyard."

"Oh, in the summer when we can use GiGi's new outdoor space."

"And all your friends and employees get to fly to Italy again."

She smiled. "They will love that."

Rico stood there, waiting for more. Technically, she'd just agreed to marry him. He was holding his son. The woman who'd changed his entire view of life was his.

He knew it in his heart.

He felt a click, something that felt like surety, like surrender, but in the best way possible.

He returned the baby to his little bin and eased himself onto her bed. "I love you."

Her eyes filled with tears. "I love you too. Ridiculously. I'm sorry it took me so long to see it."

He leaned down and kissed her. But the brief kiss wasn't enough and their tongues twined as he let his hands slide along her arms.

"Someone should call your parents."

She pulled back. "Juliette probably already has." She gasped. "Our condo's too small for them to stay with us. We need to make a reservation at a nice hotel for them. That way they can stay for weeks and we'll all remain sane."

He laughed. It was the kind of problem he'd never thought he would have. But today it was like music to his ears. He'd buy some good bourbon and invite Lorenzo and they'd sit on the terrace of the condo, watching the traffic on the street below, talking about life.

It didn't compare to Texas longhorns, but this was their home now. Manhattan. They might be frequent visitors of Texas and Italy, but this would always be home.

His life really did stretch out before him as happy, content.

He had all the things he'd told his sixteen-year-old self didn't exist.

But now he knew they existed. In abundance. With the right person.

EPILOGUE

THE DAY BEFORE Rico and Marietta were supposed to fly to Italy to help GiGi prepare for their wedding, Rico got a call from Ethan, asking him to meet him at the coffee shop. He thought it odd, considering that Ethan would be seeing him in a week for the wedding celebration, but Ethan insisted.

Twenty minutes later he and Marietta left Mikie with the nanny and walked into the coffee shop that smelled like fresh blueberry muffins and strong beans for brewing.

They got their coffee at the counter and sat across from Ethan at a small table.

Ethan slid a manila envelope across the table to him. "I wasn't ever going to show you this."

Rico frowned. "Show me what?"

He took a breath. "Long before I met you, I was a doctor."

A little surprised, Rico cocked his head. "How did you end up being an investor?"

"I invented a little instrument that became essential in open-heart surgery. Made a mint. Quit work. Became an investor." He paused. "I was a doctor in *Spain*."

Odd feelings clenched Rico's stomach at the way Ethan accented the word *Spain*, but Marietta frowned. "I know you're going somewhere with this, sweetie, but we're not picking up on it."

Ethan drew in a long breath. "One extremely cold night, when I was closing up, a young woman came into my office. She was already in labor." He shook his head. "No. She was delivering the baby. I barely got her to a table. The whole thing took a minute and a half. I cared for her, wrapped the baby in a towel and left the room to call an ambulance to take her to a hospital and when I got back she was gone."

"My mother." Rico's voice fell flat. The words felt heavy, wooden.

Marietta eased her hand over to his.

Ethan sighed. "I'm fairly certain, you were the baby I delivered that night. A week later, there was a story that went around town about a baby left in a train station. The station with in a village was twenty miles north. So it apparently took a week for the news to filter down to us, but the timing worked."

Mariette gasped. "You really think that was Rico?"

"Yes."

"So you knew my mother?"

"No. I didn't know her, and she never gave me her name. She also never named you. She was gone when I returned to fill out the birth certificate. So, I don't know much more about you than that your mom was no older than fifteen. She could have been fourteen for all I know. She'd told me that she'd hidden her pregnancy from her family… That was why she didn't want to go to a hospital. That's probably also why she ran away and couldn't take you home."

"Her parents didn't want me?"

"Her parents didn't know about you. She was a very scared, very young woman who believed she'd made a huge mistake and was trying to fix it."

"So my dad's not a mobster or in a gang?"

Mariette snorted, but Ethan chuckled. "Not that I know of. But your mom held you as if you were a precious jewel when I handed you to her. I could see in her eyes that she loved you."

Rico nodded. He'd been a father for nine months. He'd never before felt the emotions he had when he held Mikie. He couldn't imagine leaving him, but he also wasn't fifteen, afraid, probably broke. In the eyes of a teenager, letting him go might have seemed like the best option. Just as Marietta had speculated.

But his entire body rattled. Knowing who he was, or who he might be, filled him with emotions so strong, he didn't know how to process them.

"I had a friend in the foster care system. I kept track of you." Ethan laughed. "Until you moved to London. Then I lost you, so I had a private investigator find you for me."

"All those rides I gave you where you taught me about investing? Was that to make up for me being abandoned?"

"And to get to know you." He shrugged. "I wasn't a hundred percent sure you were the baby I delivered that night. And I never felt comfortable telling you the story."

"Until now."

"I've never known you as anything other than an ambitious young man. Struggling. Pushing. Now, you're stable. I thought you could handle the information. Especially since I don't believe you were unloved or unwanted. Your mother looked at you with such love. But she was a kid, who for some reason couldn't tell her parents. She was young and her decision was rash because she was desperate."

Ethan nodded at the big envelope. "That paper has all the information I'd filled in for the birth certificate. That gives you the date and time and the place you were born. But no names. Still, a good private investigator might be able to find your mother."

"It would screw up her life."

"Maybe. Or maybe she's been waiting for you." He said, "Yeah. Maybe," then folded the envelope so he could stuff it in his big jacket pocket. He would hire a private detective and make a few discreet inquiries, but if he found his mother was happy, he probably wouldn't disturb her. He had a good life, a life rich with people and purpose. Everything he needed.

* * * * *

If you missed the previous stories in
The Bridal Party trilogy,
then check out

It Started with a Proposal
Mother of the Bride's Second Chance

And if you enjoyed this story,
check out these other great reads
from Susan Meier

Fling with the Reclusive Billionaire
Claiming His Convenient Princess

All available now!

HARLEQUIN
Reader Service

Enjoyed your book?

Try the perfect subscription for Romance readers and get more great books like this delivered right to your door.

See why over 10+ million readers have tried Harlequin Reader Service.

Start with a Free Welcome Collection with free books and a gift—valued over $20.

Choose any series in print or ebook. See website for details and order today:

TryReaderService.com/subscriptions